9/27

The Case of the Dead Winner

FATHER DOWLING MYSTERIES
by Ralph McInerny

Her Death of Cold
The Seventh Station
Bishop as Pawn
Lying Three
Second Vespers
Thicker Than Water
A Loss of Patients
The Grass Widow
Getting A Way With Murder
Rest in Pieces
The Basket Case
Abracadaver
Four on the Floor
Judas Priest
Desert Sinner
Seed of Doubt
A Cardinal Offense

The Case of the Dead Winner

A FATHER DOWLING MYSTERY
FOR YOUNG ADULTS

Ralph McInerny

St. Martin's Press
New York

 For information, address St. Martin's Press, 175 Fifth Avenue, New York, N.Y. 10010.

ISBN: 0-312-13038-4

First Edition: June 1995

10 9 8 7 6 5 4 3 2 1

For Ellen

The Case of the Dead Winner

1

Edna Hospers, director of the parish center, found old Mrs. Mortimer seated in her outer office, her face ashen, her breath coming in gasps. She looked as if she had just crept into the room and collapsed on the chair. Her eyes, when she looked up at Edna, were wide and bright. At the moment it was easy to believe that, like a drowning person, her whole long life was passing before her mind. Edna pulled another chair toward her, sat, and took Mrs. Mortimer's hand in hers.

"Are you all right, dear? Can I get you something?"

Mrs. Mortimer indicated her purse. "Pills."

Edna snatched up the purse, opened it, and was confronted by a cornucopia of contents. But then the mottled hand of Mrs. Mortimer reached in and came out with a plastic vial, which she handed to Edna. "Two," she whispered.

Half a minute later, the pills swallowed, the glass returned to Edna, Mrs. Mortimer looked, if not perky, at least much better. Edna tried not to show her relief. That one of the old people who came to the parish center each day might fall ill, even die on the premises, was always a possibility. Indeed, statistically it was a probability.

Nonetheless, during the five years she had managed the center, Edna had not yet been witness of a death. There had been scares, the calling of an ambulance, an old person whisked off to the hospital. Once there had been a body on the front steps when Edna came to work, but all these tragedies had taken place off stage, and it was Edna's prayer that her luck would continue, although it was strange to think of the luck as hers. It was a great relief to see the color return to Mrs. Mortimer's cheeks and her breathing subside to a normal tempo.

"Thank you, Edna. You mustn't think I came to put on such a performance."

Edna rejected this description of what had happened. Mrs. Mortimer sipped a little more water and told of how she had become dizzy in the hallway.

"I was on my way to see you. I *am* here on purpose. But this just happened on the way. I found myself halfway between the auditorium and your office. A dilemma." She smiled. "Do you know the story of Buridan's ass, Edna? I know it sounds naughty, but it is actually a problem in logic."

Edna wanted the old woman to keep talking. Listening, she remembered that Elizabeth Mortimer had had a distinguished career as a university professor. By the time she told the story of the ass who had found itself equidistant between two piles of hay and starved to death, she was as lively as Edna had ever seen her.

"What are the pills for, Liz?"

"*The* pills?" Mrs. Mortimer had taken her purse from Edna, and now she opened it again. "I feel I should have a pharmacist's license, carrying around all this medicine."

"What's wrong?"

Mrs. Mortimer dipped her head and looked at Edna over her glasses. "Age, my dear. Growing old. And there are no pills to cure that."

How old was Mrs. Mortimer? In her late seventies, Edna supposed, surely not eighty. She had been coming to the parish center now for over a year, having only just heard of it, much to Father Dowling's dismay. Mrs. Mortimer had been in the hospital; he was informed that he had a parishioner who was a patient, he stopped by. They were of course old acquaintances, if not friends, but in the course of the conversation Mrs. Mortimer mentioned how time sometimes hung heavily on her hands, whereupon the pastor mentioned the center, the use to which the parish school had been put when there were fewer and fewer young families with children to warrant keeping it open.

"I never heard of it," Mrs. Mortimer replied.

"Don't you read the parish bulletin?"

"Father, I assume that you make all the important announcements from the pulpit."

From that point on, Father Dowling had included a weekly mention of the center, to which all senior parishioners were welcome five days a week. Edna organized programs, there was a van in which visits to local museums and galleries, or shopping trips to malls, were made. On the premises, there was shuffleboard, bridge, less demanding card games, and simply the opportunity to talk. It was a low-key operation, deliberately kept simple.

Mrs. Mortimer was an avid bridge player and had become a regular in the silent, serious games that went on in a corner of the former school gymnasium, now become the all-purpose setting for the bulk of the center's activities.

"I came to ask a question."

"What is it?"

"Someone suggested that I just approach Gerry, but I thought I should talk with you first. After all, he does work for the parish."

Gerry Krause was the nephew of Captain Phil Keegan of the Fox River Police Department and was working at St. Hilary's for the summer, mowing lawns, watering the grass, trimming shrubs, odd jobs. With Edna's daughter Janet, Gerry had become essential to the smooth running of the center.

"What did you want to ask Gerry?"

"My lawn is laughably small compared to what he takes care of here, of course, but it does need cutting. I am determined to stay in my own home, but I can really do nothing myself toward keeping it up, and I don't want the neighbors to regret that I am staying on."

Edna smiled. She was sure that the neighbors were delighted to have so distinguished a person still living among them.

"And I need a little grocery shopping done as well. Once a week, twice at most."

"You wanted to hire Gerry?"

"Edna, you must know how difficult it is to find a young person for such little tasks anymore. I understand that. More attractive jobs are available. But I wondered if Gerry would be interested. More important, I wondered if you or Father Dowling would think that I was poaching on your territory." She smiled, and her eyes drifted away. "Poaching. Do you know the word?"

"Poached eggs?"

Mrs. Mortimer's laughter was musical. She put a hand on Edna's. "Forgive an old teacher's impulse to instruct. May I talk with Gerry?"

It might have been a scene in one of the novels Mrs. Mortimer read when she wasn't playing bridge. Her reading, she had confided, was all but confined to nineteenth-century fiction. "Not only did I teach them, I loved them. I still do. George Eliot, Thackeray, Dickens, Trollope. Trollope is my favorite." She had lent Edna a Trollope novel, but Edna had found it too slow moving to hold her interest. There was such elaborate fanfare before the young man could convey to a young woman his romantic intentions. Mrs. Mortimer was more influenced by what she read than she herself might have realized.

Edna did not want Liz Mortimer to hire Gerry to cut her lawn and run an errand or two. How would she ever stop others who might reasonably want to do the same thing? On the other hand, she did not want simply to say no.

"Do you have a mower?"

"Oh, yes! And the store is just a block away. I don't think he would find it too demanding."

"What would you think of asking a boy of twelve to do it?"

"Edna, Gerry is the only boy I know to ask."

"I have a son twelve years old."

Mrs. Mortimer hesitated. "Edna, I hate to say it, but I don't remember what a twelve-year-old is like. How old is Gerry?"

"Fifteen."

"Almost as old as Janet?"

Janet was fifteen, too. Of course, at that age girls always seemed older. "Mrs. Mortimer, I will bring Carl tomorrow, and if you want to talk to him, fine, if not, fine. I won't tell him, so that he won't expect anything in case you decide against it."

"You'd really not like me to ask Gerry?"

Edna explained her fear of setting a precedent that others might want to invoke.

When she walked Mrs. Mortimer back to the auditorium, the old woman was clearly restored from the attack in Edna's office.

"Do you know I think it was in part anxiety over what I came to ask you."

"Mrs. Mortimer, you embarrass me. I hope I don't seem such an ogress."

"Edna, you are an angel of mercy. It isn't that. But I would like to have someone around the house on the days I'm not here."

"I understand."

But Edna wasn't sure she did understand. Mrs. Mortimer didn't live in an unsafe neighborhood. Could it be that she just wanted someone who could summon help in case she had an attack? Edna wondered if she should have proposed Carl. Perhaps it would have been better simply to deflect Mrs. Mortimer from asking Gerry and let it go at that.

On the other hand, she knew how Carl would welcome a chance to make some money.

2

When Father Dowling stopped by the school to look in on the senior citizens at the parish center, Edna Hospers drew him aside and told him of Mrs. Mortimer's inquiry.

"Is Gerry willing?"

"I discouraged that, Father. Imagine the result if everyone felt they could offer Gerry odd jobs."

He could see how it might interfere with the work Gerry did at St. Hilary's. On the other hand, he sympathized with an old woman's need to find someone to cut her lawn and run an errand or two. Was Edna right to think this would start a trend?

"I suggested to her that Carl would do almost as well."

Carl was easily the brightest of the three Hospers children, in Father Dowling's unexpressed opinion, and a favorite of his own. He was something of an electronic genius, seemed to suffer no ill effects of his father's being a prisoner in Joliet—of course that was largely to the credit of Edna—and was one of the most reliable of the altar boys. Summer weddings and funerals could pose a problem, but boys Carl's age were unlikely to be tied up with summer work. Carl had always responded to requests that he serve. Weddings, of course, were scheduled well in advance, but funerals were another matter. Father Dowling had come to appreciate the reliability of Carl Hospers.

"Great idea. What did Liz say?"

"That she hasn't any idea what a twelve-year-old boy looks like. I told her I'd bring Carl tomorrow and she could ask him or not as she likes."

"Won't Carl be disappointed if she doesn't?"

"I won't tell him what's up."

"Ah."

"I'll tell him I want him to change the toner in my laser printer. He's done that before."

Father Dowling nodded in deference to such maternal wisdom. There was no point in getting Carl all excited about the chance of a job if there was only a fifty-fifty chance.

"Is there any reason why Mrs. Mortimer should feel uneasy about living alone, Edna?"

"Well, I imagine when you reach her age, the thought of needing help and not having it near is unsettling."

"I suppose that must be it."

"You don't sound as if you believed that."

When Edna told him what had led her to think Liz Mortimer disliked, perhaps even feared, living alone, Father Dowling did not see it. He had known her long before he was called to the hospital on her behalf. Indeed, her husband had still been alive when Roger Dowling became pastor at St. Hilary's. Barely alive. His had been the first funeral Father Dowling had conducted as pastor. So it was as a widow that he had known her. She was already retired and had asked him to attend a meeting of a reading group when it met at her house. They were reading *Kristen Lavransdatter* and thought he would have intelligent things to say about Scandinavian Catholicism before the Reformation. He had never read the novel before and accounted it one of the major blessings of knowing Liz that he had read it.

Every time he spoke with her seemed a treat for the mind, and this had been as true when he visited her in the hospital as on all previous occasions. She was sharing a room with a woman who professed to take comfort in the fact that all the components of her body would be recycled and continue their existence in other earthly entities.

"That's the only next life I understand," she said somewhat belligerently.

"Next for whom?" Liz asked.

Father Dowling had let the two women carry on the discussion. He did not want Liz's roommate to think he had come to prey upon her in her hour of weakness. Besides, he had the notion that Liz would be more successful in distinguishing the spiritual from the bodily than he would have been.

"She had a spell in my office, Father," Edna said.

"Spell."

Edna's description of the ashen, gasping old woman was vivid. Doubtless that had given her a fright. Religious faith did not take away the fear of death, after all, and she might have had an intimation of what her last moments would be like. That could easily have carried over into the discussion of hiring Gerry.

"Where is she now?"

"Probably playing bridge."

And so she was, frowning over her fanned cards, totally absorbed in her game, like her three companions. Was a game still a game when played so intently? Father Dowling had a feeling all four of them would say it was no game at all if played any other way.

The roar of the tractor mower with Gerry at the wheel moved the priest quickly along the walk to the rectory. Why didn't they put mufflers on tractors? The other morning he had been wakened by the sound of a saw, a crew having arrived at seven o'clock two blocks away to clear away a tree felled by a storm. The whine of their saw seemed to penetrate the very marrow of his bones. He felt that his limbs were being amputated. The tractor mower was not quite that bad, but it was a noise very difficult to ignore. He got inside the air-conditioned rectory and pulled the door shut with relief.

"Gerry mowing?" Marie Murkin asked, apparently without irony.

The priest paused, cocked his ears, narrowed his eyes. "I think so."

"I thought I heard the tractor." If Marie were kidding, she gave no indication.

"Either that or the sonic boom of a low-flying jet."

Marie nodded, humming, obviously not registering what he said. How much of conversation was simply a musical exchange, he wondered, reassuring sounds whose meanings were unimportant?

"What do you know about Elizabeth Mortimer?"

"Has something happened?"

"Why would you think that?"

"Why? The woman's been in and out of the hospital, and how old is she?"

"In and out of the hospital? She was there once."

Marie looked wise. "That's how it starts."

"It?"

Marie let her eyes roll ceilingward and emitted a sigh. Father Dowling half resented this suggestion that Liz was on her last legs, even though she'd had what Edna called a spell just an hour ago.

"She wants to hire someone."

"For what?"

"Oh, just helping around the house. Washing, dusting, making beds. Windows, too, I suppose. Interested?"

Marie glared at him. "Why don't you put it in the bulletin?"

"That you're taking the job."

She stomped off to the kitchen, shutting the door noisily behind her. Father Dowling had only a moment or two of enjoyment before he felt contrite. He pushed open the kitchen door.

"I'll tell her she can't afford you."

"What's she paying?" Marie asked, quick as a shot, and he withdrew, letting her have the last word.

There was no point in telling Marie about Liz Mortimer's interest in hiring Gerry or of Edna's proposal of Carl as substitute. If something happened, she would be able to think he had already told her. If nothing did, she would dismiss the little exchange as just more of his teasing.

The trouble was that Marie Murkin had reminded him of his aunt Ruth from the first moment he saw her, and when her mannerisms and cheerfully gloomy view of life matched his deceased aunt's, he could not resist talking to Marie as he had to Ruth. With his aunt it had been tease or be teased, or maybe both, but he had to give as good as he got or stop seeing her. But visiting her had always been great fun; her mordant view of things and jolly conviction that the world was going to the dogs never failed to pep him up. By contrast, he felt like the wildest of optimists. The one time he had told Marie she reminded him of his aunt Ruth, she had taken offense, as if it were simply more of his teasing. So of course that was what it had become.

"Until she was diagnosed and put away, she lived with us. If you can call it living."

"I'm not interested."

"That's what she always said. That's why she kept her money in the toe of a slipper in her closet. My dad told her that at the bank it would earn three percent interest . . ."

But Marie had left the room. That remained her ultimate weapon. Retreating to her kitchen or, more decisively, up her own back stairs to her quarters above.

In his study, he glanced at the clock: an hour before his mass, which he said every day at noon. He filled his pipe, lit it, and settled behind the desk, reaching for his current reading. He opened the book and, puffing contentedly, began to read. The sound of the mower came to him, but he was able to keep it off to the edges of his mind.

What did distract him was the hope that Liz Mortimer would give Carl Hospers the job. He supposed that a little more money coming into the Hospers home would always be welcome. Earl Hospers had gone off the deep end some years ago and was serving a very extended sentence in the prison at Joliet. That had left Edna with three children, two girls and Carl. Janet was helping her mother this summer in the parish center, and this summer Anne Hospers had a thriving kid-watching business, taking toddlers off their mothers' hands, able to look after half a dozen at once. Carl was the only one unaccounted for, and while he was the kind of kid who could happily spend all day on the computer Father Dowling had let Edna take home when they changed equipment at the parish center, it bothered Edna to think of her son home alone for much of the day. Of course, Anne was in the neighborhood, and either Janet or her mother or both found an excuse to look in at the house during the day, but it would simplify things enormously if Carl had the kind of job Liz Mortimer proposed.

The doorbell rang, and who else but Elizabeth Mortimer was shown into the study by Marie.

"Would you like a cup of coffee, Mrs. Mortimer?" Marie asked.

"I see it's on," Liz said, indicating the pastor's Mr. Coffee.

"I wouldn't let you touch that brew," Marie cried. "You wouldn't sleep for a month after a sip of that."

"Actually, I would prefer tea."

Marie approved and went off to make some.

"How are you feeling, Liz?"

She turned her head slightly. "Why do you ask?"

"I understand you had a little spell this morning."

"Is that what it was? For a moment I was certain I was about to die. Word gets around fast, doesn't it?"

"Edna mentioned it when I was over there this morning. You were completely wrapped up in your bridge game when I left, or I would have said hello."

"I prefer talking to you here. Father Dowling, how responsible is a twelve-year-old boy?"

"Carl Hospers?"

Liz laughed. "Is that the boy's name?"

"It is. And I recommend him wholeheartedly. He is one of the brightest, most responsible kids his age I know."

"I don't know when I last saw a twelve-year-old. I have nothing to go by. I don't want a child."

"Carl is not a child."

She had come to ask his advice, but Father Dowling was not sure he convinced her that Carl Hospers was fully capable of doing the tasks she wanted done. Carl would have to make his own case the following day. And he would not even know that he had been entered in a contest.

3

Janet and Anne talked as if he had some advantage being the youngest kid in the family, but Carl would have liked to know what it was supposed to be. Or sometimes he was supposed to have an unfair edge because he was a boy, although this was usually Anne rather than Janet. But then Anne planned to rule the world despite the fact that she was a woman.

"You're a girl."

"I mean when I'm emperor."

"Empress."

"I'll empress you with a baseball bat, Carl."

Well, she didn't like to be corrected any more than she liked the fact that he got better grades.

"Things are getting easier," was her explanation. "Now when I was in fifth—"

"You were a year older than Carl."

"I'm two years older."

"You know what I mean."

"I know what you said."

Actually they got along pretty well. Not having Dad with them made it harder, but it brought them all closer together. Carl had felt very depressed when his mother explained to him about his father, about being in prison and all.

"He killed someone?"

"No. No, he didn't. It looked that way. . . ."

Carl hated to put his mother on the spot. What she was telling him was not what the jury had believed, that much was for sure, and he could imagine someone listening to his mother and saying, Oh, sure, of course she isn't going to believe her husband did a thing like that. Carl put his arms around his mother, to stop her from explaining. She didn't have to explain it to him. He was part of this family, too.

One of his dreams was that when he grew up he would prove that his father had been innocent and there would be a public apology and maybe a ton of money to make up for all those lost years.

"He wasn't innocent, Carl. He did things he shouldn't have done. Crimes. But he did not kill anybody. If he were only paying for what he did do, he would have been home long ago."

It was a tough subject, and they didn't have to mention it out loud for it to be there. Maybe they never really forgot it. Carl, when he turned his mind to it and thought of his father sitting in a cell as the weeks and months and years went by, felt that that image had been there all along. In his subconscious.

"Subconscious?"

"Thinking about U-boats."

Anne threw a pillow from the sofa but missed. She seldom missed, but then she was laughing when she threw it. Anne's comment on his mother's insistence that he come to the parish center with her and Janet was typical.

"I told her I'd have to charge if she expects me to be looking after you while she's gone."

The truth was that the days went by a lot quicker than even Carl himself believed possible. For one thing, he spent most of his time in front of his computer, an old IBM relic his mother had brought home from work. It had been one of the oldest, with two floppy drives, a model prior to the XT, what Father Dowling had called a Model T.

"What's a Model T?"

"An ancient Ford. But indestructible. Like the DC-Three."

Carl knew about airplanes, so he got that one. He had put in a hard drive to replace one of the floppies and had added speed and a graphics board so that he could run more sophisticated programs.

"Games," Anne said, making a face.

Sure, games. But Father Dowling had gotten some meatier software for him—an astronomy package that could absorb Carl for hours, a logic program that was pretty much like a game. Carl would have liked to add a CD drive and get into some of those huge databases, but that stuff ran into real money. Meanwhile he was having a great time with his modem, keeping the calls local so his mother wouldn't have a heart attack when the phone bill came. There were scads of bulletin boards in the Chicago area, and he had downloaded some pretty sophisticated communications programs. A few weeks ago he had recovered a program erased from the computer of a man who had tried to get two other guys into trouble. It turned out that Timothy Walsh had been stealing money that the other guys had stolen, only they had been to prison already. Walsh was awaiting trial, and Carl had been interviewed by a local channel; a newspaper reporter had called him on the phone, but if he wrote anything about the case, no one had seen it.

He had told his mother that he could put new toner in her printer in about two minutes, so why didn't they go over tonight and just get it done.

"Not tonight, Carl."

"Janet can drive me over, Mom. Really, it's no big deal."

"Hey, Carl," Janet said. "How about a little cooperation, okay? Mom says tomorrow, let's make it tomorrow. You got a date or something?"

"Sure," Anne said. "He's going swimming with Gerry." She said this in a singsong voice and then got out of the room fast, but if Janet was mad, she was also smiling.

So he went to bed early, and the next morning when his mother woke him up he had forgotten all about going to work with her and just said, "Good-bye, Mom. I'm getting up."

"You bet you are. And hurry. I am a punctual woman."

Then he remembered and was out of bed and barreling for the bathroom.

Carl saw the parish plant on weekdays every once in a while, but that was when Father Dowling called on him to serve as an altar boy. Going to the school with his mother, standing there while she unlocked her office and following her in, made the whole place seem different. Already cars were arriving, bringing the older people for whom the parish center had been founded. They were through working, retired, and had stayed put where they had lived, not going off to Arizona of Florida or somewhere warm, and the center gave them a place to get together.

"Where's the toner, Mom?"

"It should be in the closet."

Carl rummaged around in the closet for a while, but he was darned if he could find the toner. His mother had gone off somewhere, so he looked around himself for likely places where she might have put it. If it turned out that she was out of toner, Janet could take him to a computer store in the van. There was a job he'd like to have when he got his driver's license, getting behind the wheel of that van. He turned at the sound of his mother's voice.

"There's no toner in the closet, Mom."

"Carl, this is Mrs. Mortimer."

Carl shook the woman's hand, being careful not to squeeze it. She really looked fragile. How old was she, a hundred or so?

"So you're Carl."

He looked at his mother, but she gave him no clue. Carl felt she was putting him up for sale and Mrs. Mortimer was about to make a bid.

"You're much bigger than I would have thought, Carl."

There wasn't anything to say to that.

"He may be a little large for his age," his mother said, her voice sounding different from the way it did at home. "Why don't the two of you sit down and talk. I have to check out the auditorium."

And his mother sailed out of the office. Mrs. Mortimer sat down, but Carl stayed on his feet. He was beginning to see that his mother hadn't brought him here today to take care of her printer. He was here to meet this lady, and he had no idea what was going on.

"Do you know Gerry Krause, Carl?"

"Sure."

"Yesterday I asked your mother if she thought Gerry would have time to do a little work around my house. Well, she didn't like that idea. And she suggested you."

"What kind of work?"

"Good." She nodded. "Always ask a direct question."

Carl listened to her while she told him of mowing her lawn and going to the store for her once in a while.

"I come here to the center several times a week. I would like to hire you on the days I don't come here. That way I'll be home and we can talk about what work you'll do. Are you interested?"

Interested? Carl felt as if he had suddenly been promoted several grades at school. When the summer started he hadn't any idea of getting a job. There had been talk of a summer course at a local college for kids, but they hadn't made a decision on that yet. Now to be asked if he would like a job made him feel as old as Gerry. Mrs. Mortimer had wanted Gerry and now she wanted him, so that put them on the same level, sort of.

"Yes."

"Just yes?" Mrs. Mortimer didn't look as old as she had. Her smile was nice, and for a moment Carl could imagine her as a girl. Oh, she was old, but she wasn't ancient.

"I'd like to work for you."

"Good. I want you to." She put out her hand again, and they shook. "I thought I would pay you twenty dollars a week. If there should be any extras, well, I'll pay you more."

Twenty dollars? Already he was figuring how many weeks he'd have to work to buy a CD drive. It was a little disappointing to realize that he couldn't make enough money even if he worked for the rest of the summer.

"But I'll check that with your mother, to make sure that's fair."

"Oh, it's fair. That's plenty."

He didn't want her thinking about it, maybe changing her mind. Making money was only part of it. He wanted a job.

His mother, of course, wasn't surprised when he told her. She had found the toner now, and Carl took care of the printer, ran off a few things to make sure it was working as it should, and that was it.

"What am I supposed to do the rest of the day?"

"Janet will drop you off at the house. She's taking a van load to the mall, and there should be room for you."

Meanwhile he fooled around with the computer in his mother's office. Not much on it, a spreadsheet, a word-processing program, and that was it. Yet it was a powerful machine, one of the first of the 486s, which was unlikely to be made obsolete soon. It made him want to get back to his own machine. There wasn't much left of the original machine now except the case, but the main thing was that it had a slew of resident programs and he had others he just loaded up when he wanted to use them.

It was more than an hour before Janet got her group ready to go. Carl had spent some time in the auditorium, thinking he would kibitz, but the old people weren't used to having someone his age around. He was asked how old he was and what grade he was in half a dozen times before he escaped outside. Gerry was laying hose on the lawns in preparation for watering. A few games of shuffleboard were going on, real cutthroat, old geezers who looked as if a stiff wind would blow them over were putting all the steam on it they could when they sent the puck down the court, trying to knock off the opponent's scoring points.

Three women and a man were going shopping. The man wore a straw hat and suspenders and treated Carl as if they were in league against the women. But Carl could see that whatever the man said to him was directed at the women, who ignored him yet seemed to hear everything he said.

"These gals are going to get first-degree plastic burns from using their credit cards. Do you know what's worse than a woman on her way shopping?"

"The man tagging along with her," one of the ladies said, not looking at him.

"A lady coming back from shopping." The old guy cackled as if he had told a real joke. The women made smacking disgusted sounds. But then Janet hopped in, closed the door, and started the motor. Everybody gripped a pole as if they were about to go off on a roller coaster.

Actually Janet drove with great care, never exceeding the speed limit, taking the corners without much tipping, always signaling the move she was about to make. Carl had been on the alert to catch her in some infraction, but there weren't any. He had studied the manual when she took driver training, and while he had no actual time at the wheel, he was certain he could handle the van.

"You're going the wrong way," the old man called out to Janet, and the ladies began to chatter nervously.

"We'll drop my brother off first. This is my brother, Carl."

The old man put out his hand. "I thought you were Father Dowling."

"How old are you?" an old woman asked.

"What grade are you in?" asked another.

For the rest of the ride he had to answer dumb questions. He wished he'd answered with sign language and let them think he was deaf and dumb. But Janet wouldn't have let him get away with it.

Carl hopped out at the house and hung around while Janet drove away, to give everyone in the neighborhood a chance to see how he had come home. He walked slowly toward the house, conscious of the fact that he had a job now.

It was a distracting thought, and he found it hard to settle down to the computer. Finally he looked up Mortimer in the phone book and got out his bike. It seemed a good idea to look over the place where he would be working tomorrow morning.

4

Mrs. Mortimer had a daughter, Alice, who lived on the near north side in Chicago and almost never came to see her, which was all right with Mrs. Mortimer. It was a sad fact of her life that she had never gotten along with her only child. Her husband, Harry, had spoiled Alice, giving in to her constantly, never saying no, with predictable results. Of course Harry never noticed the results of his indulgence because Alice was as sweet as could be to him. Mrs. Mortimer had to bear the brunt of her daughter's lack of discipline and found herself cast in the role of the bad witch while Harry was Santa Claus. Alice had rebelled against her mother's intellectual interests and, although she had high potential, barely made it through high school. College, of course, was out of the question. College was her mother's domain. Alice went off to seek fame and fortune in the Loop.

Harry had felt terrible when he found that their daughter was a cocktail waitress in a downtown bar, but what else could she do? By then Alice no longer took the trouble to behave differently to Harry than she did to Mrs. Mortimer, and they saw less and less of her. When Harry fell seriously ill, Mrs. Mortimer had trouble reaching her daughter, and by the time she did, Harry had already sunk into a coma. It was a time when they all might have been reconciled, but alas that did not happen. After the funeral Alice drove off, pleading the necessity of being at work at four, and since then their communications had been almost exclusively by telephone. Mrs. Mortimer sometimes wondered if she would ever speak to her daughter at all if she didn't telephone Alice.

Suddenly, out of the blue, a month ago, Alice had called. Nothing in particular, just to talk; and two days later she'd called again.

"Is everything all right, Alice?"

"With me? Of course. How are *you* doing?"

Such concern for her health was unprecedented. Mrs. Mortimer hadn't told Alice of her stay in the hospital a year before. The spell she'd had yesterday in Edna Hospers's office had not been the first such episode. It would be too much to say they were regular. Of course, she was frightened. She would spend every weekday at the parish center, but it was a chore getting there, and once she was there she found she had so little energy, it was all she could do to stay awake. That was when she'd thought of having someone at the house.

An obvious move would be to hire a day nurse, perhaps advertise for an au pair or companion her own age. Mrs. Mortimer found that she could not do that. It would be like an announcement that she was no longer quite able to look after herself. It was her intention to live out her days in the house she and Harry had shared. Memories of her daughter were not pleasant, but her love for Harry had not diminished, and she missed him terribly. It was noticing Gerry mowing at St. Hilary's that had suggested another possibility. If she had a reliable boy around the house several days a week, doing odd jobs but basically just being there, she would feel more secure and it would not appear that she needed such reassurance.

Would anyone have imagined that Professor Elizabeth Mortimer would have been as anxious as she was when she went to ask Edna Hospers if she could approach Gerry? Her heart was pounding from the moment she left the auditorium, and climbing the stairs had seemed a feat of physical strength. Coming down the corridor to Edna's office, she suddenly had difficulty breathing and was afraid she would black out. How she got into the office she would never know, but she managed to fall onto a chair, and then Edna was beside her, helping her. Not a very auspicious beginning to the conversation. And when Edna demurred, Mrs. Mortimer was extremely disappointed. She was wishing she had asked Father Dowling rather than Edna, when Edna suggested her own son.

Of course, Mrs. Mortimer was wary. She really had no idea what a twelve-year-old looked like anymore. She tried to remember Alice at that age, but the only image that formed was the expression of indifference on Alice's face at her father's funeral. Now that she had met Carl she was completely at ease, quite confident that he would do. But it seemed ominous that Alice had telephoned her again last night.

"This is becoming quite a habit, Alice."

"I think of you there all alone."

Mrs. Mortimer laughed. "Oh, you mustn't dramatize my situation. I am going from morning to night."

"I tried to call you earlier."

"This is my bridge day."

"Where do you play?"

"Oh, we move around."

There were two tables at St. Hilary's at which bridge was played, and it was true that some days Mrs. Mortimer played at one table and some days at the other. Alice's concern was so out of character that Mrs. Mortimer felt she didn't owe her a complete report.

"Will you be home this weekend?"

"I could be. Is there some reason . . . ?"

"There's someone I want you to meet."

Mrs. Mortimer's heart melted, and she felt awful for the skepticism with which she had received her daughter's questions of concern. Alice was now in her late thirties, she had never married, and Mrs. Mortimer had come to think she never would. "I'm having too much fun," Alice had said to her father whenever he had asked if there was any special man in her life. Mrs. Mortimer had found that a singularly joyless answer. Did her daughter intend to remain a teenager for life? Harry had died with the sad certainty that he would never have a grandchild. And here was Alice with excitement in her voice, asking if she could bring someone to meet her mother that weekend. They settled on Sunday.

Now, with the prospect of Carl spending several days a week at the house, the whole project seemed less compelling to Mrs. Mortimer. Perhaps if she had waited a day, that call from Alice would have driven the idea from her mind completely.

5

Marie Murkin was happy to hear that Carl Hospers would be doing odd jobs for Mrs. Mortimer, though why the pastor treated the news like a world-shaking event she did not know. The rectory housekeeper would have rejected with scorn the suggestion that there was anything remotely like jealousy tainting her attitude toward Edna Hospers. She would not, of course, have drawn attention to the great misfortune in the Hospers family that had led to Earl Hospers's arrest and conviction for second-degree murder.

"Since there was no murder, he could not have committed it," Father Dowling said with annoying certainty.

"I refer to the official judgment."

"The trial? It is scandalous that such happenstance was admitted as evidence."

Perhaps. Marie knew that Phil Keegan, the Fox River captain of detectives, thought about as much of Father Dowling's effort to exonerate Carl Hospers as she did. Well, there was no need to rub it in. After all, a priest should judge for the better if anyone should, no matter the facts of the case. As for Edna, well, it sometimes helped to remember that she was a woman to be pitied, particularly when the pastor seemed to forget it.

"I'm sure he will be a great help to her."

"Weren't there any Mortimer children?"

"Only one. A daughter . . ." Marie paused, swishing her dust wand about, the picture of distracted indifference. She wouldn't say another word unless he asked. She would not give him the chance of calling her a gossip.

"A girl?"

"Well, a daughter. She would be a woman now. Not even a young woman anymore."

"Where does she live?"

Marie pulled out a chair and sat down. This was an opening big enough to drive a truck through, and she did not intend to ignore it. Besides, she had an obligation to keep the pastor informed about his parishioners, particularly when he had acted as employment agent for them.

Marie remembered when Alice Mortimer still lived at home, an absolutely spoiled child, Daddy's girl. It was all the more noticeable because of Mrs. Mortimer's professional success. Even in those golden days of St. Hilary's parish when there had been a large number of professional people in the parish, a college professor had been a novelty, particularly a female college professor. You would think that a girl with a mother like that would take after her, but Alice Mortimer had been her father's girl and seemed to rebel against any suggestion that she might follow in her mother's path. In fact, she had been a terror, running with a wild crowd, actually written up in the paper for underage drinking when a party was raided.

Marie had breathed a sigh of relief for the Mortimers when Alice moved to the Loop.

"Doing what?" Father Dowling asked.

"Working in some bar."

Again she waited, not wanting to volunteer information, but she was started now and might just as well give him the whole story, even though Father Dowling pursed his lips and began to lift the morning paper from the table where he had dropped it.

"She never married."

"I'm surprised you know so much about her, Marie."

"Oh, I don't think anyone knows everything there is to know about Alice Mortimer."

Like it or not, he was going to hear the story, and she would put it as delicately as she could. There had been rumors, and the pastor could check them out with Phil Keegan if he liked, that Alice was connected with a very low crowd indeed. But what was to be expected when she had worked in bars and nightclubs all her life?

"Maybe what she's looking for is a substitute for her child," Marie said, assuming a thoughtful tone. She spun around and glared at the pastor when he laughed.

"Marie, spare me your pop psychology."

"I was giving you my mom psychology."

And she huffed out of the study, thundered up the back stairs to her room, and sat on her flouncy chair with closed eyes, trying not to think angry thoughts about the pastor. What a trial that man could be. Oh, it had been foolish letting that remark escape her as soon as the thought occurred to her. But turning it over now, brooding over Father Dowling's reaction, Marie found her explanation even more plausible. And she thought of something else as well, something that made a connection between Mrs. Mortimer and the Hospers family seem almost inevitable.

It wasn't that Harry Mortimer had been a crook or criminal, but he had been a gambler, wasting more time than a serious man should at the track. In those days you had to go to the track if you wanted to gamble legally. Now there was a subject for a sermon, not that Father Dowling ever took her advice on these matters. There was a time, and not too long ago, when there had been a shame attached to gambling. Father Dowling might dismiss this concern and say it was only Methodists who worried about gambling and drinking, not Catholics, but she knew what he thought of the lottery, forever developing new games to separate people from their money. And now, with the waterways of the state thick with floating casinos, Chicago wanted to turn Navy Pier into another Las Vegas. Honestly.

When Mr. Mortimer was rumored to be a regular at the racetrack, it had been said in whispers, mentioned as shameful; it was certainly not considered an ordinary and innocent way to pass the afternoon. That didn't make him an Earl Hospers, of course, and for the rest, he was a respectable man. Still, Marie could imagine Mrs. Mortimer sympathizing with Edna Hospers. Nor when she dwelt upon it did she find it implausible that Mrs. Mortimer was half adopting the Hospers boy, not just employing him for odd jobs. Marie Murkin knew a thing or two about the human heart, no matter the mockery of the pastor of St. Hilary's.

6

Going by the house on his bike, first several times on the front sidewalk and then through the alley behind, gave Carl some sense of where he would be working; but it wasn't until Wednesday, when he actually started and Mrs. Mortimer was there to greet him and show him what she wanted him to do, that he really believed he had a summer job.

"The mower is in the garage. Would you get it out?"

There was a bench on the back porch, and she sat while he went out to the garage. He had seen it from the alley, a two-car frame building that didn't quite match the house, which was stuccoed. The big surprise was that the floor of the garage was unpaved, just packed dirt that gave off a nice smell of old oil and grease as if time had just stopped there. Carl bet that if he closed his eyes, it would be easy to imagine old cars here, maybe even one of those Model T's. There was no car at all. A push mower was tipped up and leaned against the wall of the garage. When Carl pushed it out into the sunlight, its blades spun, moving easily. Where the axle met the wheels grease was visible.

"I hope you weren't expecting a power mower like the one at St. Hilary's."

"In a yard like this?"

"What's wrong with the yard?"

"Nothing. But it's just a small yard. This mower is all I'll need."

"I don't know how sharp the blades are."

"It looks in good shape, Mrs. Mortimer. Look at that grease."

She started to lean forward, then drew back, smiling. "I'll take your word for it."

She sat there watching as he got started, but after he had gone back and forth a couple of times, the porch was empty. Carl liked that better. He didn't want her watching him. How could he just work then? Besides, the blade was dull, and he noticed grass that had been flattened rather than cut rising up again. He cross-mowed to take care of that, but he would have to take a file to those blades and sharpen them up.

He got to like that push mower from that first day. Unlike a power mower, it took energy to keep it moving, and he worked up a satisfying sweat. It got so that when he was in the sunlight, he looked ahead to getting into the shade, but once there, he pushed on in order to come into the sunlight again. It was important not to get the job done too quickly, as if it didn't really amount to anything. It turned out that Mrs. Mortimer thought he was working too fast.

"Carl, you're wringing wet. Sit down and drink this lemonade. You make me feel that I'm breaking the child labor laws."

All the tools in the garage were mechanical: the clipping shears, the trimmer, the fertilizer spreader, whose propellerlike blade was moved by the wheels and sprayed fertilizer in wide arcs on either side.

"I'm just trying it out," he told Mrs. Mortimer when she looked surprised to see him directing the fertilizer back and forth across the backyard.

"My husband made a big fuss about the yard. He had a green thumb."

At first Carl thought she meant this literally and waited for an explanation. But when she talked of her husband's roses and vegetable garden, he figured out that that was what she had meant.

"I can't keep plants in the house. Before I retired, I always forgot to water them. Now I suppose I water them too much. Whatever, they never last. Harry could make a desert bloom." She looked around. "Once this yard was the talk of the neighborhood."

Carl resolved to make it that again. It made the job more than a job. Mowing the grass and doing a bit of trimming might have been just keeping things the way they were. Now Carl had a goal. And he could see, now that she had mentioned it, that the borders had been overgrown, that hidden away among weeds were flowers that didn't have a chance in their present condition. That led to another goal. Carl promised himself that he was going to learn about flowers and gardening, he was going to be able to identify plants and trees accurately. Why, this wouldn't be just a job, it would be like going to school.

* * *

His first week, Mrs. Mortimer decided to stay home Thursday and Friday, too, and not take part in the programs for seniors at the parish center.

"So I'll be here if you have any questions."

Carl would have liked to be alone, now that he knew what the job was, but Mrs. Mortimer did not continue the close supervision of his first hours on the job. On Thursday he more or less forgot that she was in the house and might be looking out at him. The job itself got all his attention. Wednesday night he had crammed on gardening and asked Gerry, who was over visiting Janet, for advice.

"Carl, all I do is cut the grass, water it, and keep the weeds back. At least I think that's what I'm doing. I'm not always sure that something's a weed."

"Then what do you do?" Janet asked.

"Let it be."

"Until the last judgment?" Anne asked, and everyone looked at her. "The story in the gospel? Oh, come on, you know what I mean."

Carl went to his room and searched some of his CD's and began printing out articles he thought would help him with his job at Mrs. Mortimer's. It hadn't been clear at first, but it turned out that she wanted him to come in the morning and stay through the afternoon, so that on the three days he worked for her, he left home when his mother and Janet drove off to St. Hilary's and got back just before they did.

"Of course this means I'll pay you a good deal more than we talked of at first."

She asked what the minimum wage was and said she

would pay him that. Carl had it multiplied and added in his mind in a flash and could hardly wait to buy the current copy of *Computer Shopper* and start looking up electronic bargains. It was on Thursday morning that the couple came.

The car came slowly along the street while he was trimming the grass along the curb. Carl smiled at the lady on the passenger seat, since she seemed to be watching what he was doing, but she didn't smile back. The car pulled into the driveway, but only far enough to block the sidewalk. Carl kept on clipping, looking at the car. The lady was turned toward the driver, and they sat there talking, as if they weren't sure why they were there. Finally Carl went over to the car, figuring they might need some help.

"You lost?" he asked.

The lady did not turn. Maybe she hadn't heard him. Carl bent down and looked in, and his eyes were locked with the driver's. They were the deadest fish eyes Carl had ever seen.

"What the hell do you want?" the man asked.

The woman turned and jumped when she faced Carl. He asked again if they were lost, but now the question sounded kind of dumb, given the fish eyes of the driver.

"Lost? Who are you?"

"Carl Hospers."

"What are you doing here?"

"I work here."

She tucked in her chin, and now her eyes looked fishy. Then she smiled, but it only involved one half of her mouth, sending one corner up. She looked as if he had told her a joke.

"No kidding." She opened the door and got out. With

heels like that, he thought, she'd better not walk on the grass. "Is my mother home?"

"You mean Mrs. Mortimer?"

The man had gotten out of the car, too. Carl would have expected him to be nine feet tall, but he could barely see over the top of the car. He wasn't much more than a head taller than Carl. He was a head shorter than the girl, but then she was wearing those heels.

Carl hadn't known Mrs. Mortimer had any family, but this woman didn't look at all like Mrs. Mortimer. Her jaw worked as she chewed gum, and there was a cigarette in her long-nailed fingers.

"What's your name?"

"Carl."

"Oh, yeah, you said."

Not very flattering. On the other hand, she now spoke to him as if they were old friends, as if they were the same age, as if she found the man she was with as funny as Carl did. A door slammed and she looked toward the house, and there was Mrs. Mortimer standing on the front porch. Carl waited for her to recognize her daughter and show it with a smile, but she just stood there, waiting, until the woman went toward her, walking the way Janet did when she kidded around, the heels noisy on the driveway.

Carl looked at the man, who was looking at him across the roof of the car.

"I'll wait," he called after Mrs. Mortimer's daughter.

"Come on, meet my mom, Sal."

Sal? There was a song Janet had learned, a Johnny Cash tune, "A Boy Called Sue." Well, here was a man named Sal. Somehow it didn't seem a joke.

7

It had gladdened Elizabeth Mortimer's heart when Alice had telephoned and then repeated the deed, signaling that at long last their estrangement might be coming to an end. Had she thought of Alice as a girl when once again she heard her voice? Did she imagine that they could go back to some point in time before daughter had distrusted mother and mother was disappointed in daughter and start all over again? If that had been her thinking, Mrs. Mortimer received a rude shock when she came onto her porch and recognized that the woman talking to Carl Hospers was her daughter, Alice.

Her first reaction, before she saw that it was Alice, was to protect the boy from this brassy woman who had shown up preposterously in her driveway. The shortness of the skirt, the height of the spike heels, the working of the face as she chewed her gum, suggested a kind of woman boys like Carl should be shielded from.

"Mom, how you doing?"

Then she saw it was Alice swinging up the drive, her purse bouncing off her hip, a large false smile on her face. The man with her, short, furtive, his eyes darting about, seemed an all-too-appropriate companion for Alice. Mrs. Mortimer felt suddenly sick at heart.

The man's name was Sal. He nodded at what was an identification rather than an introduction and stood a step or two behind Alice when she brushed her mother's cheek with her lips and then stepped back. Her eyes swept over the house.

"You'd think the house had been declared a historical site or something. Time stood still here, huh?"

Mrs. Mortimer held open the door so that Alice and her friend could enter. Carl still stood at the foot of the drive, next to the car in which Alice had come, silent witness of the reunion of mother and daughter. That this was a reunion brought Mrs. Mortimer to life, and she went in to make her guests welcome.

Alice said sure, why not when Mrs. Mortimer suggested tea. "I think Sal would rather have a drink. Right, Sal?"

He tipped his head and lifted his brows.

"A drink."

"You probably don't have anything in the house, do you? Give him a beer."

"I don't have any beer, either." For a wild moment she thought of sending Carl to the store for beer, but of course they would not sell it to him. "There's some wine."

Alice laughed. "Wine, good. Give him some."

"I don't want no wine."

A double negative. Of course he did not mean what he said—namely, that he wanted wine. It was doubtless meant as a refusal.

"We'll all have tea," Mrs. Mortimer said. "Just make yourself comfortable and I'll have it ready in no time."

When she left the living room, she passed the front door, and through the screen came the renewed sound of the trimming shears, Carl back on the job. This was why she had wanted to hire Carl; that was clear to her now, whatever excuses she might have given herself and others. She did not want to have to face her daughter alone. What defense against Alice Carl could be would be difficult to say, but his presence was a reassurance to her. In the kitchen she ran water into the kettle, put it on the stove, and then stayed where she was. A watched pot may not boil, but the time went by all too quickly as she tried not to eavesdrop on what was being said in the living room.

Alice spoke in a whisper and was answered by inarticulate grunts. It was absurd, but Mrs. Mortimer felt fear at the muffled exchange, as if the two of them were plotting against her. Alice's pointed reference to the house might have been laying claim to her inheritance. Was that what had brought her back, the prospect of gain? This was easier to believe than that Alice had been moved by daughterly sentiment, or by that alone, when she telephoned. Was it possible that she had heard of the stay in the hospital after all? Had someone told her that her mother looked old and ill?

The steam of boiling water set the kettle whistling, and that brought Alice into the kitchen, an odd little smile on her face.

"How the sound of that kettle brings it all back." She stood in the middle of the kitchen, hands on her hips, and looked around possessively, Mrs. Mortimer thought. "I can't get over how unchanged this place is."

"I've always liked it as it is."

She had never thought of altering it, redecorating. That

would have been as bad as moving out, putting a definitive end to her life with Harry.

"My room the same, too?"

"Go up and see. But not until you've had your tea."

Her friend Sal took the cup and saucer Mrs. Mortimer handed him, separated the saucer from the cup, put the saucer on the table, and eyed the contents of the cup. Alice laughed at him without embarrassment, taking good-natured delight in his discomfiture.

"I'll bet you wish you'd taken that wine."

He sipped tentatively. "Geez, that's hot."

"I should have served iced tea."

"Mom, it wouldn't matter. Don't worry about it."

Alice's remark gave her credit for feelings she did not have. She resented rather than sympathized with Sal's reaction to her tea. Surely he must have noticed the steam lifting from his cup. She felt dreadful. Her prodigal daughter had returned, and she could not wait for her to leave and to take Sal with her. Sal was the problem, she insisted to herself. If Alice had come alone, it would have been different, a reunion, not this awkward meeting over unwanted tea. But it was difficult to think that even alone she could discover her lost Alice beneath the brassy, wisecracking exterior.

"Who's the kid?"

She meant Carl. "A neighbor." He was, in a way.

"There still families living here?" Alice twisted her face into an exaggerated expression of disbelief.

Had the neighborhood changed so much? Mrs. Mortimer wondered. There were fewer children now, certainly, and they were likely to be grandchildren. Father Dowling said the trend was reversing, but Mrs. Mortimer did not say this to her daughter. It would have sounded apologetic, as if she were ashamed of the neighborhood in which she had lived most of her life.

"You should get a condo and not have to worry about things, the yard, maintenance, all that." Alice's hand made a vague comprehensive gesture.

"Do you live in a condo?"

A harsh laugh. "Not quite." She turned to Sal. "When Dad bought this house it was some place, let me tell you."

Sal just looked at her. Was he Alice's boyfriend or what? Mrs. Mortimer stopped the thought. It was best not to wonder about the life Alice led.

"What'd he do?"

He meant Harry. "He was in sales," she said carefully.

"Yeah?"

"A manufacturer's representative." That was the legend he usually had put on business cards, as if the printed words could make it a reality. He worked only to acquire sufficient money to gamble. When Mrs. Mortimer met Harry he had been a graduate student in mathematics, interested in the theory of probability. His interest in gambling had begun as a result of his research. And then he had become addicted to it. Mrs. Mortimer had read Dostoevski's "The Gambler," she had lived with Harry, but she had never understood the compulsion to gamble. It wasn't like taking a chance in the lottery or playing bridge for a penny a point. Gambling as Harry had engaged in it had little to do with money; it was as indifferent to winning as to losing. It was a form of suicide.

"Leave him," Coburn, the chair of her department, had advised when she had unwisely confided her troubles with Harry to him when putting the case for a raise.

"He's my husband."

"It sounds a lot more as if you're his caretaker."

For better or worse she had married Harry, not believing at the time that life with him would be anything but good. But it wasn't simply a bargain she had made and meant to stick with. She loved Harry. And, it turned out, Coburn's interest in her was not simply professional friendship. His wife had died in childbirth, and the baby too had died, leaving him doubly alone. He was a great solid man whose specialty was Elizabethan literature, which, he said without a smile, was what attracted him to her.

"Wasn't Queen Elizabeth bald?"

"Only in the movie."

She adopted a kidding tone with Richard Coburn as a way of keeping him at arm's length. Not that he wasn't a perfect gentleman. It was all too easy to imagine a far different life with him, rid of the perpetual worry and concern that Harry represented. But how could she ever put Harry completely out of her mind? So she had stayed with Harry and they had grown old together and now she was alone. Richard Coburn stayed in touch. A year ago he had called to tell her he was moving to a retirement apartment.

"I can't imagine you retired."

"Perhaps because you imagine the place otherwise than as it is. You must come visit me."

"You come visit me. If they ever let you out."

He told her all about Greenlawn. She much preferred her occasional days at St. Hilary's Center and living in the house that had always been hers. But now with Alice and Sal filling the living room, she felt like fleeing.

Eventually they left, and Mrs. Mortimer tried not to let

the relief she felt show. There had been no announcement of an impending marriage, so that had not been the purpose of the visit. Yet Alice had wanted her to meet Sal. Why?

Carl was working in a flower bed at the far end of the yard and kept his head down until the car had backed out the driveway and went away up the street.

8

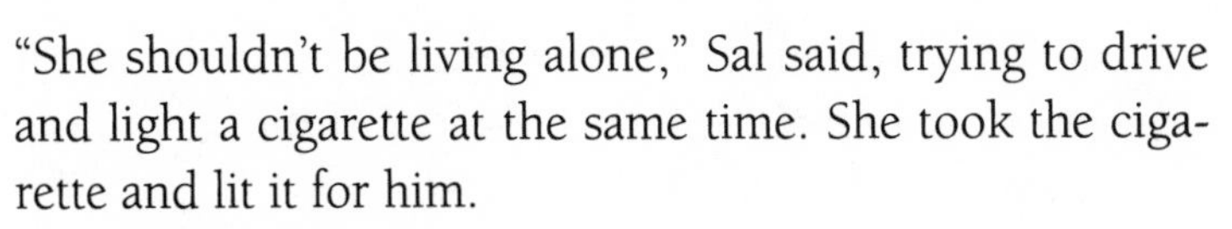

"She shouldn't be living alone," Sal said, trying to drive and light a cigarette at the same time. She took the cigarette and lit it for him.

"Maybe I should move home."

"Would she let you in?"

"Are you kidding?"

Alice had felt good about visiting her mother, even if her motive was what it was. Sal just wanted to get a look at her, that was all. Sal had known her father. No wonder. Sal wasn't a gambler, not like Dad had been, but he made his living off those who were. When Sal first asked about her mother, he acted surprised that she was still living in the old house.

"I thought she'd be living in Florida or Arizona, someplace warm."

Sal thought a condo in the sun was a good investment: use it yourself, rent it when you weren't there. He looked at her slyly when she said her mother was a retired teacher. Sal seemed to be waiting for her to say more.

"Sal, do you know what a professor retires on?"

"No, but I know your father got lucky."

"He was never lucky in his life."

"You're wrong."

She let it go, mainly because she had the thought that Sal's interest in her was not what she had taken it to be. He had found her attractive and fun, he liked to be with her, that was what she had thought; but from the time he asked about her mother she knew there was something else. She brooded over his remark about her father's luck. Finally she asked him.

"Hey, ask your mother. Ain't she his heir?"

"Any money my father ever won he lost."

Sal just shook his head. The amount he spoke of was staggering and involved long-distance betting she did not understand.

"After he paid the taxes it was still a bundle. The shock must have killed him."

The date Sal mentioned was just months before her father's death.

"You think all that money went to my mother?"

"Unless your father buried it somewhere."

That turned out not to be far wrong. Sal discovered that her father had rented a safe-deposit box about the time of his big win.

"But wouldn't that have been opened when he died?"

"Who's Elizabeth Rush?"

"That's my mother's maiden name."

"The box is in her name."

Did she know it? Was her mother in possession of that kind of wealth, buried away in a bank vault, not even gaining interest, living as simply as she always had? It was impossible not to see how fragile her mother looked when she visited the house with Sal. What would happen to that money if her mother should die? She talked with a lawyer Sal recommended, a man named Tuttle, who took off his tweed hat when she introduced herself and was about to put it on again when he thought better of it. He sailed it toward a coat rack in the corner and missed.

"Forget it," he said."

"I wasn't going to pick it up." What kind of a clown had Sal sent her to? But Tuttle proved cagey enough when they got down to cases.

"In the hypothetical situation you mention, such a box would be sealed after the death of the renter and would be disposed of when the will is probated."

"The will."

"Isn't there a will?"

"What if there weren't?"

"That complicates matters. It might be some time before the money was released to the heirs."

"How much time?"

"No more than a few years," he said carefully.

"Years!"

"Of course a shrewd lawyer could speed things up."

"Meaning you?"

"Is this a hypothetical case, Miss Morton?"

"I'll let you know."

"He who hesitates is lost."

"That's catchy."

"I got it in a fortune cookie."

Was he serious? It was hard to say. There was a man sitting in the outer office who reminded her a bit of Sal. Tuttle introduced him as Officer Pianone.

"Fox River police."

"He under arrest?" Alice asked, pointing to Tuttle.

Pianone had Sal's sense of humor, too. He just stared at her.

"Keep in touch."

"What do I owe you?"

"Why don't you run a tab?"

There was no secretary. Did he do his own bookkeeping? Where on earth had Sal heard of a lawyer like Tuttle? And what did it mean that there was that clod of a cop sitting in his outer office?

Alice had looked into the matter of safe-deposit boxes. The renter was given one key and the bank had another, and both were needed to open the box. There were several possibilities. Either her mother knew of the money and had a key to the safe-deposit box or her father had never told her of it. In either case, that key had to be somewhere, and where else but in the house?

The next time Alice visited her mother she was alone. The kid was in the yard, but her mother wasn't there.

"She went to St. Hilary's."

The front door was locked, but when Alice went around to the kitchen door, she found it open. She stepped inside and stood in the kitchen. On the visit with Sal she had not really felt that she was in the house in which she had grown up. His being there seemed to shut out the past. But now, alone, listening to the sounds of the house and, from the yard, the sound of a mower, she was transported back to when she had been a girl. She felt almost dizzy and opened her eyes but had to steady herself on the stove.

The mother she remembered now was not the old woman she had visited a few days before, but a much younger woman, a successful professor, who very much wanted her daughter to follow in her footsteps. Alice didn't know when she first realized that her father was very different from other men his age. He was loads of fun, far more fun than her mother, but he was like a kid. When he was home. He was away a lot. "On the road," was the explanation, but there was something about her father that was a secret she wasn't supposed to learn.

She had a friend whose father drank, but that wasn't it. Her father smoked constantly, but that seemed the extent of his vices. That and never being home for very long. It was when he pawned her mother's rings and Alice couldn't shut out the argument that she learned that her father was a gambler. He had gotten some money for her mother's rings and lost it all on what was supposed to have been a sure bet.

"It was just borrowing," he said, his voice sounding subdued after her mother's angry tone. "It was just on loan."

"Then where is it? Where are my rings?"

Eventually her mother bought her rings back, but from then on Alice looked on her father with a mixture of pity and contempt. He no longer had any authority over her. His example suggested to her that a life could be thrown away, wasted, and this both horrified and fascinated her. In the end, she supposed, she had thrown her own life away. Sal represented a chance of starting over. The large sum of money her father had won just before his death would come to her, it would be her dowry, she and Sal could move away and start over. But even as she thought it, Alice feared this was a wild dream.

For years she had learned not to expect much from

others, not really to trust them. In her world everyone looked out for number one, and friendships were simply ways of doing that. Sure Sal was attracted to her, they had fun together, despite his inability to really loosen up; but Alice did not kid herself. If Sal hadn't heard of her father's winning and assumed she had access to the money, nothing would have happened between them. This realization did not gladden her heart. She countered it by telling herself that she was just using Sal to break free of her life in Chicago. There she was a waitress, and that was all she would ever be, running her legs off until she dropped. Somewhere else, anywhere else, with Sal and a little money, almost looked like heaven.

She had gone from the kitchen to the living room and then went upstairs and stood in the doorway of her room. Tears came then, she couldn't stop them. She was overwhelmed by the sadness of things. So short a time ago she had been just a girl, listening to her parents quarreling about her mother's pawned rings. She wanted to sit on the bed and have a good cry, but she didn't. She wiped her eyes and straightened her shoulders. The money her father had won belonged to her. They owed her at least that much.

Where was the key to the safe-deposit box? She went through the jewelry box on her mother's dresser, carefully removing and replacing the rings and necklaces, bracelets, earrings. She removed the little tray and rummaged through the odds and ends covering the bottom of the box. There was no key.

Sal had told her to look for a red cardboard envelope with the name of the bank on it.

"They snap shut. Like this." He took such an envelope

from the coat of his jacket and gave it to her. "Open it."

Inside was a flat key. That was what she was looking for. It wasn't in the jewelry box, it wasn't in the top drawers of the dresser, among the lingerie and hankies, it wasn't in any of the drawers. There was a little table beside the bed. As she was going through it, Alice noticed the rosary hung over the bedpost. She thought of her mother telling her beads before she dropped off to sleep. Did she pray for her wayward daughter? Alice was sure she did. It was a comforting thought.

But she was angry that she could not find the key. In the closet she checked pockets of dresses, searched the shoes to see if something was hidden in the toe of one of them. She looked everywhere she herself might hide a key, but she did not find it.

9

The nice thing about working in Mrs. Mortimer's yard was that it left Carl's mind free. Oh, he put his mind to what he was doing, he was very careful using any kind of tool, particularly the shears, but that still gave him the opportunity to think of other things.

He was in correspondence by E-mail with someone named Juan in Guadalajara who apparently taught school but whose English was imperfect. Carl hadn't told Juan that he was twelve years old, only that he was a student with a hobby in landscaping. The correspondence wasn't about him, anyway, but mainly about computers. Juan had an old Apple he had upgraded and an external modem that sounded the size of a toaster. Juan was a new entry on Carl's list of computer correspondents. He kept the long-distance calls to a minimum, using a network as much as possible. He had persuaded his mom to sign them up on CompuServe, promising that he would pay the monthly fee.

"Oh, I think I can afford it, Carl."

"But you don't use it."

"Maybe I'll start."

"You really ought to have a computer at home."

"That I can't afford. Won't you let me use yours?"

"Sure."

It was hard to tell whether she was kidding or not. But they signed on to CompuServe, and Carl checked in for mail in the morning before leaving and the first thing when he got home at night.

Almost as much fun was tapping into the Fox River police databank, to which he had been given the code by Lieutenant Horvath.

This morning it was hard to think of anything but the yardwork and the fact that Mrs. Mortimer's daughter, Alice, was in the house even though Mrs. Mortimer was away.

"I hadn't seen her in years," Mrs. Mortimer said after the man and woman had driven away.

"Is that her husband?"

"No." Mrs. Mortimer said it as if the idea scared her. Carl was glad. The eyes of the man were scary. Salvatore Bianco was the name on the registration Carl found in the glove compartment.

Since coming to work for Mrs. Mortimer, Carl saw that he was kind of her protector as well. She didn't want to be all alone in her house, and she didn't want to go to the St. Hilary's Center every day. He could have kept the lawn in good shape by spending a few hours a week on it, but now she wanted him to come every day. Well, not *every* day. Today he could have stayed home because she was going to St. Hilary's, but he liked the idea that he had an everyday job. Besides, he was beginning to make progress on the flower beds with which he was edging the lawn. If he were being paid by the hour, he would have felt he was taking advantage of the old woman, but she had to pay him only twenty dollars no matter how often he came. That morning she had almost decided to stay home.

"I didn't realize you were coming. I should have told you I mean to go to St. Hilary's today."

"You did. That's okay. I've got plenty to do."

"I'm going to pay you by the hour."

"No, that's okay. It's not really work, you know."

Finally she did decide to go, and Carl was glad. He felt more in charge when he was there alone. And then the daughter, Alice, came.

She waved in acknowledgment when he told her her mother wasn't home, and Carl watched her try the front door. He hoped she would go away when she found it was locked, but she went around the house and time passed and he knew she had gone in the kitchen door.

What was she doing in there? It wasn't as if she lived there or visited a lot. Mrs. Mortimer had told him it had been years since she had seen Alice. At least Salvatore Bianco hadn't come back here.

Carl had typed that name on his computer when he was fooling around with the Fox River police databank, just on a hunch. Sal's eyes were the eyes killers in stories had; there was something menacing in his bulk. So it didn't really surprise Carl to discover that he had a police record. A long one. Sal was forty-one now, and the first entry was many years ago, when he would have been a kid: auto theft. His offenses as a minor had only earned him probation, and it wasn't until he was twenty that he spent time in jail, the Cook County Jail. The last entry was almost a year old, merely an arrest, no follow-up. Sal had been questioned about the death of a man named Welsheim. Carl made a note of it.

The next day after leaving Mrs. Mortimer's he stopped at the main library and found the Welsheim case in the microfilms of the local papers. He had a printout made; why not, as long as he had looked it up? The body of Eugene Welsheim had been found in his automobile. His automobile had been found in the Chicago River, spotted by a pilot who was tracking the course of the river. The only speculation about the death was that Welsheim was a known gambler whose debts had in the past earned him several beatings. The story faded from the paper after three days.

That night Carl checked the investigation of the Welsheim death—it had never been officially called anything other than a death—and found that Salvatore Bianco was the only one who had been questioned about it. Bianco's connection with illegal gambling was noted.

What did it mean? Who knew? Carl thought about telling Mrs. Mortimer her daughter had come home for a visit with a known criminal, but that didn't seem fair. As far as he could tell, Bianco hadn't done anything wrong for years. The questioning about Welshiem was only that, questioning. Maybe Alice intended to marry the man. Telling Mrs. Mortimer about the man's past activities would turn the old woman against him. Carl thought about his own father and tried to feel protective of Salvatore Bianco. Then he remembered those cold, dead eyes and it was hard to think that man needed protection from anyone.

It was over an hour before Alice came out of the house. She didn't look too happy.

"Where'd you say my mother was?"

"At St. Hilary's. The center."

"Oh, yeah. What's it like?"

"The center? My mom runs it."

"No kidding."

She didn't sound impressed.

"You going over there?"

"Maybe I will."

After she was gone, Carl went inside and called his mother to tell her to be on the lookout for Mrs. Mortimer's daughter.

"I told her she was there."

"I didn't know she had a daughter."

"Her name is Alice."

"I'll look for her. Does Mrs. Mortimer know she's coming?"

"I don't think so."

He hung up. He hadn't told his mother about the visit of Alice and her boyfriend to the Mortimer residence.

After that call, Carl went through the house, wondering what Alice had been doing inside all that time. Cleaning up? But Mrs. Mortimer always kept the house neat as a pin. Her phrase.

"Neat as a pin?" Carl repeated the first time she said it.

Mrs. Mortimer smiled at him. "No, I don't know the origin of the expression. It means very neat. Everything in its place. Spotless."

That described the house all right.

Mrs. Mortimer came home early in the afternoon, just as Carl was getting ready to go. He waited for her in the driveway, hand on the seat of his bike to steady it.

"I understand I had visitors today."

"Your daughter, Alice, was here."

"So she told me." Mrs. Mortimer seemed about to say

more but hesitated. "Did you let her in the house, Carl?"

"The back door was unlocked."

The old woman thought about it. "I must have forgotten." She shook her head and made a noise. She looked at Carl. "Alice doesn't have a key to the house."

Carl did. It was on the ring of keys along with the key to the garage and an extra set of keys to a car Mrs. Mortimer no longer owned.

"I didn't leave it unlocked, Mrs. Mortimer."

She was surprised by his remark. She came and put her arms around him, but he didn't mind. She looked as though she would break in two, yet she was a strong person, Carl was sure of it. She was saddened that he thought it was his fault his daughter had gotten into the house.

"Would you find it odd if I asked you whether Alice took anything with her?"

"I don't think so."

"A terrible question to put to you, I'm sorry."

"I would have noticed, Mrs. Mortimer. I didn't like her in the house when you weren't here."

"Did she go out to the garage?"

"No."

"Well, we'll just keep the doors locked from now on. I mean I will," she added quickly.

Riding home, Carl pondered her question about the garage. So Alice was looking for the envelope Mrs. Mortimer had had him hide in the garage.

10

Cy Horvath had been on the Fox River police force ever since it was clear that his athletic career was going nowhere. He had been a high school star, the subject of rave pieces in the *Sun Times* and *Tribune,* to say nothing of the Fox River paper. There had been speculation about the number of scholarships he would be offered, but he wasn't leaving the state, and IU came through and everything looked great. Until he broke his leg. While it healed, other players pushed ahead of him, and at the end of the season his scholarship was taken away. He couldn't afford to stay in school. Phil Keegan found out he was driving a delivery truck and came by to see him. The dispatcher went wild, wanting to send Cy out on a delivery, but Keegan just looked at him.

"Buzz off." He showed the dispatcher his badge.

"He'll think you're arresting me."

"How's your leg?"

"Good enough for this kind of job."

"Any chance of going back to school?"

"To study, sure. Not to play football. No one would take a chance on me now."

"Gleason."

"Yeah."

A local sportswriter had wondered in print whether Cy Horvath didn't have the football equivalent of a boxer's glass jaw. All the skill and strength, but brittle bones. The writer was just guessing, but it was the killer blow to Cy's career.

"You're good enough for the Bears right now."

"That sounds like Gleason, too."

Keegan hesitated, then laughed. Gleason was notorious for putting down local teams. If he had said Cy was ready for the Bears, it would have been meant as an insult.

"You're big enough to be a cop."

He was bigger than Keegan, but the captain of detectives had the look of a half-back, smaller and lighter, maybe, but able to play with the big boys. Cy waited until Keegan said what he had to say. It sounded a lot better than driving a truck. Keegan took the ignition key, walked over to the dispatcher, and dropped it into his palm.

"You arresting him?"

"What's your name?"

"I just asked."

"Don't."

In the car, Cy said, "Well, there goes my job."

The next Monday he was in training. Keegan kept an eye on him and after six months of patrol car duty transferred him to the detective bureau, where he had been ever since. Whatever he knew about being a cop he had learned from Phil Keegan. Keegan took the place of the father Cy no longer had. He and Lydia had no children of their own, and that was hard, but there wasn't anything they could do about it. Cy showed Lydia an article about adoption, but she just pushed it away. Maybe she still had hopes. But Cy had talked with the doctor.

If they'd had kids, they might by now have a son the age of Carl Hospers. Cy smiled. It knocked him out the way Carl knew computers and had helped them figure out how Timothy Walsh squirreled away all that money. Walsh had found it pretty humiliating to be done in by a twelve-year-old kid. That was why, when Carl wanted to talk to him about Salvatore Bianco, Cy was interested.

"You want me to come to your house?"

"I'm out in the lobby, Lieutenant. I rode my bike down."

Cy got up and headed for the lobby. It was at least a five-mile ride from where the Hosperses lived to police headquarters. Carl sat at a table, his hands joined before him, watching everything that was going on. It was quite a scene for an adult, so a kid must find it pretty crazy.

"Come on to my office, Carl. This is no place to talk."

Because everyone else was talking, for one thing. Carl came along with him, and Cy slowed when he realized he was going too fast for twelve-year-old legs. In the office, Carl went immediately to the computer.

"They put that in there. I almost never use it."

"Can I try it?"

"Sure."

Within seconds the sheet on Bianco appeared on the monitor.

"I know the guy," Cy said. "Not that he hangs about Fox River much anymore."

"He's a friend of Mrs. Mortimer's daughter, Alice. Alice brought him out to meet Mrs. Mortimer."

"She's going with him?"

"I guess."

And Carl smelled a rat. Maybe he was right, but given the way Alice Mortimer—or Morton, as she called herself—had been living since she moved to the Loop from Fox River, it was no surprise that she ended up with a bum like Sal Bianco.

"Let me use that thing," Cy said, having a thought. Carl scrambled out of the chair, and Cy sat and brought up another set of records. Sal had married Sylvia Riley ten years ago. There was no record to show that they weren't still married. Of course, people got divorced almost anywhere. Cy tapped in an inquiry and turned to Carl.

"You think something's wrong, Carl?"

"I don't know. He's a real mean guy."

"You're right about that."

"And I know Mrs. Mortimer doesn't like him."

Carl was concerned for the old lady he worked for and understandably suspicious about a guy like Sal Bianco. Cy had the impression that Carl didn't care for Alice, either, but he never said so.

"After I looked the man up in your records, I could see why Mrs. Mortimer wouldn't want her daughter to be with him. Or want her to bring him to the house. But maybe he's changed. The only recent thing was an arrest for questioning."

Cy showed Carl around, knowing the kid's curiosity. He said good-bye to him in the computer room, where the woman in charge was delighted to show Lieutenant Horvath's young friend around her domain.

"Is this your nephew?"

"Yeah. Kind of."

Carl smiled from ear to ear, and Cy felt pretty good himself going back to his office.

His computer told him that there was no record of a divorce for Salvatore Bianco in any of the mainland states. Cy sat back and thought about it. Either nothing was going on between Cy and Alice or there was. If there was, either Alice knew or did not know about Mrs. Bianco. Cy bet she didn't.

He put a patrol car on it, discreetly, and the word came in the next day. Sal Bianco lived with his wife at the address in the phone book. The remaining question was whether Alice Hospers knew.

"What was he questioned about?" Phil Keegan asked when Cy went to him with it.

"That body they found in the Chicago River. Eugene Welsheim. The suburbanite who got over his head gambling and couldn't pay off."

"Wasn't Harry Mortimer a gambler?"

"I never knew him."

"Marie Murkin was going on about him the other day. It was a big hush-hush scandal in the parish. The wife a successful professional woman, professor of something or other, and the husband a deadbeat who took any money he could lay his hands on and bet it."

"How did he die?"

Keegan looked at him. "Why don't you find out, Cy."

"I'll ask Monique Pippen."

"Or Gore. He's the coroner, you know."

11

Tuttle, of Tuttle & Tuttle, sat in his office, feet on his desk, tweed hat pulled over his eyes, waiting. He was waiting for two things. First, for Peanuts Pianone to arrive with their takeout Chinese food and, second, for a bulb to go on in his head. Ever since Alice Morton, née Mortimer, had come by to ask him about how she stood as heir of her mother's property, Tuttle had felt there was something she wasn't telling him.

He had ticked off Mrs. Mortimer's apparent assets. There was the house, a nice house, but in a neighborhood that wasn't what it had been. It would bring a nice price, but nothing to retire to the Fiji Islands on. Her retirement program couldn't be transferred to the daughter, Tuttle was pretty sure of that. Savings? What could she have socked away on a teacher's salary? Besides, her husband had been a gambler.

In the warm tweed darkness of his hat, Tuttle frowned. He had been to Las Vegas once and become physically ill at the sight of grown-up human beings sitting like zombies, throwing away their money. It didn't look like fun. Most of the gamblers looked as if they were serving a long sentence rather than on vacation. Chances were that Mr.

Mortimer had squandered any money his wife had tried to save.

So why had his antennae begun to twang when the daughter came asking about her chances if there were no will? Tuttle had put a scare into her, hoping she would enlist his help to make sure she received what was coming to her. She hadn't been too informative about why she had come to him.

"A friend suggested you."

Tuttle wished she didn't look as if she wondered about the advice.

"I could make inquiries," he offered.

"Where?"

He smiled. "Professional secret."

"Let me think about it. I'll give you a call."

Sure she would. Tuttle knew he had lost a potential client when she left the office. He didn't brood about it. The woman would be lucky to get much money when and if her mother died, so there wasn't much there for a lawyer.

He eased his hat back a bit. The fact that the woman's prospects turned on her mother's death stuck in his mind—particularly given the fact that she was running around with Sal Bianco.

Bianco was a gorilla. On his own, he would have been in the slammer for life long ago, but the people he worked for provided protection and cover, and he was walking the streets as if he were a law-abiding citizen. Tuttle did not want to think of the crimes Sal might have on his hands.

Peanuts arrived with his arms full of still steaming goodies, and they settled down with paper plates and plastic silverware. Tuttle used chopsticks, not too successfully, but it impressed Peanuts.

"I been thinking about Alice Morton."

"Yeah. You in love?"

"Funny. You know who she's going with?"

"No."

"Salvatore Bianco."

Peanuts, with a mouth full of egg roll, shook his head. "He's married."

Tuttle let it ride. For a cop, Peanuts had a very cheerful view of the human race. Or he was dumb. Most people leaned to the second explanation, but Tuttle liked Peanuts and preferred to think of him as naive. Besides, he was a constant source of information about what was going on at police headquarters, and that was often a professional advantage to Tuttle. But Peanuts buttoned up about Bianco, and it wasn't just the refusal to think that a married man was being untrue. It was like trying to get Peanuts to talk about his family, whose reputation in Fox River was also pretty bad. There were some who said the family had gotten Peanuts on the force in order to have an inside man. Most people thought they just wanted him off their hands. But Peanuts was dumbly loyal to his uncles and cousins who were up to no good, and Tuttle never pressed him on the matter. Now, you would have thought Sal Bianco was a cousin or something.

"Talk about something else," Peanuts advised.

"How's your fried rice?"

"Mushy."

"Try the sweet-and-sour pork."

"It's Friday."

"That still a rule, no meat on Friday?"

Peanuts shook his head. "Friday we have pork roast at home."

"So have some eggplant."

Tuttle was on his own as far as Sal Bianco was concerned. He wouldn't have told even Peanuts what had occurred to him. If Alice Morton had grown impatient to get whatever it was her mother intended to leave her, she might be tempted to hurry the old woman on her way to the next world. If that were the case, Sal Bianco could be of help to her. Whether or not he did it himself, he could always find someone to do the job.

This was dangerous territory, and Tuttle did not want to wander into big trouble. Bianco looked pretty clean; the last thing Tuttle found on him was that he had been called in for questioning when they were investigating the death of the man who had been found in his car in the Chicago River. There had been no determination that the death involved foul play. The guy could have driven into the drink himself, having been putting the drink into himself for hours prior to his death. Tuttle found this out by making a call to the Cook County coroner, identifying himself as Detective Pianone. So maybe it was an accident. There was no way of proving it wasn't. But Bianco had been questioned because it looked like the settling of accounts with a loser who welshed on his gambling debts.

It was funny how gambling seemed to surround Alice Morton. Not that she gambled. She'd been a waitress in one Loop cocktail lounger or another for years. Maybe that was a form of gambling, too.

12

Father Dowling made a point of stopping by the center and chatting with Mrs. Mortimer after Edna said that Alice had come to see her mother.

"She upset the old lady, I don't know how."

"Marie says they've been estranged for years."

Edna did not pursue that. Father Dowling knew that there was an edgy relation between the director of the parish center and Marie Murkin. The housekeeper considered herself deputy pastor, more or less in charge of everything and everyone, and of course Edna resisted the suggestion that she should report to the rectory housekeeper.

"How's Carl working out?" Father Dowling asked, pulling up a chair next to Mrs. Mortimer.

"That boy is a marvel, Father. I can't be grateful enough that you suggested him. You know I was going to pay him just a certain sum a week, but he is so industrious I intend to pay him for all the hours he works."

"Was that your daughter who came by the other day?"

A vertical line formed on the bridge of Mrs. Mortimer's nose. "Came by here? Yes."

"I didn't even know you had a daughter."

"I might have forgotten myself, I've seen so little of Alice over the years. Mothers and daughters are supposed to get along, aren't they? Alice and I never did. She was her father's daughter."

"How long has your husband been dead?"

Her eyes drifted across the room. "It seems like yesterday, but it was years ago. Seven years. You never knew him, of course, not that you would have if you had been pastor while he was still alive. He had drifted away from the church. I won't say he lost his faith; he was the most credulous man I've ever known. He gambled, Father. He lived in the belief that a random distribution of cards, the cast of dice, some poor horse running on an oval track, would make him a rich man. But if he ever had become rich, he would have soon been poor again."

"It's spoken of as a disease, isn't it? Gambling."

"Oh, yes. Everything is. I think that's too easy an explanation. In any case, it is an acquired disease. He might have considered himself the toy of fate, but I never did. I saw him become what he was."

"He never won?"

"It didn't matter."

He did not pursue the painful subject, and talking of her daughter was more painful still. That night Phil Keegan came by, and while they sat in the study, smoking and Phil, at least, drinking beer, Father Dowling brought up the subject of Mrs. Mortimer.

"Funny you should mention him. Cy Horvath brought him up the other day, at least he brought up his widow and daughter. You know Carl Hospers?"

"Of course. Edna's son. He's helping Mrs. Mortimer with her yard this summer."

"Quite a kid. Computer freak. Cy gave him the code to call in to our databanks, and the kid told Cy he had chased down a guy named Salvatore Bianco because he had visited Mrs. Mortimer, coming with her daughter."

"I hadn't heard about him."

"A killer."

"And he's walking around free."

"There may be as many killers free as there are in prison. Maybe more. No one has ever proved anything on Bianco, but there are things that are known which can't be proved."

"Or disproved?"

Perhaps it was the duty of the policeman to be suspicious and to think the worst of his fellow man, but Father Dowling could not endorse that as a general rule of behavior. It was at least imaginable that someone whose life had gotten off on the wrong foot, as Salvatore Bianco's undoubtedly had, could mend his ways and lead an honorable life.

The address of the Biancos placed them within the geographic boundaries of St. Hilary's parish, though as far as he knew, no Bianco attended mass. Certainly there was no Bianco among the contributors to the expenses of the parish. That did not mean what it once would have; parish boundaries were no longer as binding, and people tended to pick and choose their parishes for a variety of reasons. Nonetheless, Roger Dowling felt he had sufficient reason to stop by the Bianco home and give them a pastoral greeting.

After he rang the bell and stood shivering on the doorstep, he had the feeling that he was being inspected. A full minute went by and he had reached out his hand to ring again when he heard a lock turn in the door. Locks, rather. Marley's ghost might have been rattling his chains on the other side of the door, and then it opened, just a crack, and a woman looked out, eyes widened, a timid expression on her face.

"Mrs. Bianco? I'm Father Dowling, pastor of St. Hilary's. . . ."

"We don't belong."

He shivered visibly, stamped his feet, hugged himself. The door opened more.

"May I come in?"

She unlocked the outer door with great reluctance, and Father Dowling felt he was taking advantage of her timidity. She seemed to be a woman used to being told what to do, and no one had told her what to do if a priest came to the door.

The house was furnished in a featureless expensive way, as if model rooms had been lifted bodily from the windows of a furniture store and transported here. The living room was not large enough for all the things in it. Above the fireplace was a reproduction of a Murillo madonna. Mrs. Bianco was a little woman, scarcely more than five and a half feet tall. She looked familiar. She indicated a chair, and he sat, but she remained standing.

"Haven't we met?"

She looked sheepish. "I come to mass at St. Hilary's most Sundays. I just slip in the back. Sal only goes to funerals and weddings."

"Sal's your husband?"

"We don't have envelopes, but I do put money in the basket."

Is that why she thought he had come? Father Dowling

was embarrassed to be put in the role of bill collector. On the other hand, it provided an excuse for his being here. But he could not accept this version of his call.

"That isn't why I'm here. Have you asked your husband to come with you?"

"No! You know how men are, Father."

He nodded. He had learned things about women, too, but being a priest was not like being a policeman. It was the goodness in people that struck him, even when they were not all they should be, even when they were very bad. It would be a strange view of religion to regard it as only for people who didn't need it.

"Are there children?"

"Oh, Father, we've tried. I've prayed and prayed. But we haven't been blessed. Sometimes I think we are being punished."

"Why would you think that?"

She sat on the edge of the sofa, as if she were not allowed in her own living room. Father Dowling had experience of people about to tell him everything, and that was indeed what Sylvia Bianco's expression meant. For half an hour he heard the story of her marriage. She had hardly known her husband before they were engaged, more an agreement between relatives than between her and Salvatore. They had been married ten years, there were no children, her husband was a stranger to her. She had no friends, he discouraged this, he did not want strangers in his house. But he brought no friends of his own home, either. His life was a vast mystery to her, and on the festive occasions when the families gathered, she felt as close to cousins and uncles as she did to her own husband.

The words just gushed forth, a tale that this poor woman had been dying to tell, sitting all alone in her childless house, half afraid to answer the bell, warned against striking up friendships with her neighbors.

"What is he ashamed of, Father?"

"Surely he can't object to your going to mass?"

"He's not awake yet when I go. I slip out and am back before he knows it."

"What would he do if he knew?"

She shuddered. "I don't know."

He advised her to tell her husband that she went to mass. "I will see that you meet people at St. Hilary's. He can't object to people you meet there. You should get out, be helpful to others. There are things you could do."

Her face brightened at the prospect, and she sat straighter, as if making up her mind to do what he said; but when he rose to go, he wondered if she would have the courage to break out of the prison her house had become. Was her husband really such an ogre? But now that he had made this call, Father Dowling had a basis for approaching Salvatore himself. He was certain that, face-to-face, he could break down whatever resistance the man might have to his wife's taking an active part in the life of the parish.

He drove slowly back to his rectory, pondering the mystery of human life. There were millions of families in the great Chicago area, no two of them alike, each household a different stage on which comedies and tragedies were played. It seemed sentimental to feel compassion for such a crowd of strangers; it was work enough to retain the pastoral impulse toward members of St. Hilary's, people who came within the range of his responsibility. It was comforting that God, at least, could be concerned with all the millions and billions of people on the earth, love them one at a time and each for himself alone. Father Dowling murmured a prayer that little Sylvia Bianco would be firmly in the focus of that divine concern.

When he arrived back at the rectory, Marie met him at the door, her expression indicating that someone was waiting to see him. In the front parlor sat Liz Mortimer and a powerful elderly man who, like Liz, would understand the allusion if Father Dowling told him that he looked like Sidney Greenstreet.

"Father Dowling," Liz said, her voice oddly excited, "I want you to meet the chair of my department, Richard Coburn."

The fat man gave a snorting laugh as he held out his hand. "I haven't been identified in that way for years. Hello, Father. Elizabeth has become such a fan of yours, I had to meet you."

But it was clearly a reunion with his old colleague rather than a visit with the pastor that had brought Richard Coburn to St. Hilary's. His eye softened when it went to Liz Mortimer, his manner, outwardly suave and controlled, nonetheless suggested the nervousness of a teenager with his girl. It was difficult to tell how Liz reacted to this, because of course she would have picked it up more quickly than anyone else. There were occasional autumnal, even winter, marriages among the senior citizens who came to the parish center. The major motivation was companionship, a weapon against loneliness. From time to time a special person was found and marriage entered into. Instructions for a couple of advanced age about to enter into matrimony was appreciably different from those given young people for whom a long stretch of years, children, and unpredictability defined the future. Father Dowling was not sure he had hit upon the right note with old couples. One thing was certain. The notion that marriage was a form of friendship came to the fore.

"Well," Marie Murkin said when Liz Mortimer and Richard Coburn had gone.

She said no more, waiting for the pastor to give her the green light for comment on the odd couple who had just left the rectory.

"Have you ever noticed Sylvia Bianco at mass, Marie?"

"Sylvia Bianco!" Marie was crushed to have attention diverted from the promising topic of Richard Coburn's more than friendly interest in Liz Mortimer.

"That means no."

"I don't even know who she is."

Father Dowling feigned a frown, as if Marie had failed in some duty. "That's all right."

"All right?" Marie sounded as if she were being strangled. Usually he chided her for being nosy, and now he was blaming her for not being nosy enough.

He waved his hand, as if absolving her, and went into his study. There was a noisy silence in the hall and then the exasperated slamming of the kitchen door. Father Dowling tried not to smile. He bowed his head and asked divine help to stop teasing the housekeeper. No man was tempted beyond his strength, of course, but this was a near case.

13

Liz supposed that most old people felt as she did. Until she looked in the mirror each morning, she might have been thirty or more years younger than she was. That was silly, of course. Her hair was white, her bones were brittle, there was a slight stoop of the shoulders, and her eyes had weakened. But however true that was, inside she might have been the same girl she'd been all those years before, when the future was shrouded in obscurity. Now she told herself that she was in the evening of life, in the late fall of the years allotted her. But it took convincing. Richard Coburn understood.

"I heard a man our age use a baseball metaphor. He said he had rounded third and was heading for home. But he didn't sound as if he really believed it."

Some years had passed since she and Richard had been colleagues. She had not intended to confide in him about Harry, but as chair, Richard was bound to know more than others in the department. He was brusque and matter-of-fact, and she was able to speak to him without shame of her domestic difficulties. It had taken her a long time before she'd admitted to herself that Harry was a lost cause. No one else could help him; he had to do that himself, and he was utterly unwilling to change. Cheerless as his life was—the pointless wagers, the roller coaster of wins and losses—he could not tear himself away from it. By the time she spoke of Harry with Richard, she no longer found it difficult to describe him as a lost cause.

"Leave him."

She had been startled to receive any advice, let alone this. Leave her husband? Harry might have abandoned himself, but she would not withhold the love she had pledged him. She cut that conversation short; Richard had gone far beyond the bounds in making the suggestion. He did not apologize for it.

"It is a simple matter," he insisted. "Either two people are made miserable or only one. The choice seems obvious."

"You're not married."

"No, I am not. I am a widower."

"What would you say if I suggested that you marry?"

"I would accept."

They both burst out laughing, and that ended what had been a difficult meeting. As time passed, Liz realized that it wasn't entirely a joke with Richard Coburn.

That had been too bad, because she genuinely liked him. His area was Elizabethan literature, and he was also a devoted student of the classics. How many men were left who peppered their casual conversations with lines from Horace and Virgil? He was a dramatic, popular teacher, but somewhat feared, too, as he discouraged any chumminess in students, something he considered the bane of the times.

"We are here as their mentors, Liz. We must pass judgment on their performance. This false camaraderie is meant to make our task more difficult, to *influence* us."

"You make it sound like influenza."

"It is the same word!" He was so delighted with her, she thought he would hug her. She stepped back.

"Beware of false camaraderie."

He was orating in Latin when she stepped from his office and drew the door shut behind her.

They had drawn closer in what turned out to be Harry's last months of life. And then, abruptly as it seemed, Harry was dead. A great weight was lifted from her. No more need she wonder what bad consequences for her his deeds might bring. Richard was helpful during the bad days, saw to the mortuary arrangements, contacted Alice. At the funeral, when Richard took her elbow to help her into the funeral director's limousine, Liz heard someone say, "She's not wasting any time, is she?" At that precise moment, at the depth of her grief, the thought of marrying again seemed almost sacrilegious to her. The result was that she swiftly raised a barrier between herself and Richard Coburn.

He telephoned daily, after a decent interval, asking her to have dinner, to do this or that, but she refused.

"Liz, you mustn't sit alone and brood."

"You have a very gloomy view of my social life."

He said nothing, but she could feel his pain seep through the line. As if to justify the suggestion that she was being squired about by someone else, Liz asked Willy Hanson, a widower in the English Department, to accompany her to the opera. It was their only date. Within a week Willy was found frozen to death in a snowbank flanking the parking area. There was a contusion on the back of his head, apparently caused when he'd slipped on the ice. Somehow he had crawled to the snowbank, which was to be his final resting place.

Liz was unable even to go to the funeral. Suddenly death seemed everywhere, and she wanted to flee. She arranged with the campus travel bureau to spend two weeks in Florida between semesters. On the third day she ran into Richard in a seafood restaurant. They stood staring at one another.

"I scarcely believe my eyes," he cried.

"Richard." She walked into his embrace as if they had not seen one another for years. For the rest of her stay, she saw him every day. They even had the same return flight to Chicago. Back in her house, Liz regained her bearings and half regretted the happy Florida days with Richard.

"Well, did he find you?" the toothy woman in travel who had arranged her trip asked Liz in the lounge. Liz just looked at her.

"Professor Coburn. He wouldn't take no for an answer. I don't know what he would have done if I had continued to refuse to tell him your vacation plans."

Liz dismissed it, putting the woman at ease, and returned to her office. Later Richard looked in and asked if she was busy that night.

"What did you have in mind?"

"Dinner?"

"Good."

It was time, she decided, that they had a talk. It would be impossible now just to put him off as she had done before. Their time together in Florida had given him reason to think that their relationship was something more than professional. She would have to tell him outright that she wanted things to be as they had been before Florida. She liked Richard, she enjoyed his companionship, but it was clear that he was unwilling to settle simply for friendship. In her own home, in the house where she had lived so long, Liz simply could not imagine herself married to another man. It would be cruel to say this to Richard, but it would be far more cruel to permit him to think things were otherwise.

"You begrudge me the occasional dinner, do you?"

"That isn't it."

He had assumed an air of great dignity, his manner was formal, and this made it easer. She was grateful to him.

"No, it isn't," he agreed. "I cannot conceal that from the first time I saw you I lamented that I had not met you when I was young and you were untrammeled. When you became a widow, my hopes rose. I thought I had reason to hope." He raised his hand when she tried to say something. "You gave me no reason. I do not blame you." He looked at her for a moment in silence. "If you ask me to withdraw from your life, I will of course do so. But I must also declare my love for you. It is because I love you that I will do what you ask, however painful it is to me."

It had been very solemn and very definitive. From that day on he stopped asking her to do things, he no longer telephoned, he was civil, even cordial, when they met during the day, but things returned to where they had been.

Now here he was again, and Liz found herself responding to him like a schoolgirl. Father Dowling saw what was going on, but thank God he was not amused by it. Was it really possible that she would marry again, that she would accept Richard and move with him to a new place and start a new life at her age? They could not live in her house, she would not move into his condo; they needed what Richard called a tertium quid, some third thing.

Sometimes just daydreaming about it seemed enough; it was not a real possibility, or so Liz told herself. What mattered was that she found in Richard someone with whom she could discuss Alice.

Richard remembered Alice from Harry's funeral and had some inkling then of the estrangement that had taken place between parents and child, certainly between mother and child. Having no children of his own, he should have regarded the situation as Father Dowling did, sympathetically but remotely. Richard, however, reacted with surprising emotion. He had no doubt that whatever fault attached to the estrangement was Alice's.

"Her life looks like an effort to punish you and thwart your expectations of her."

"I'm sure she doesn't give me two thoughts." But it was difficult not to take pleasure in what he said. In her heart of hearts, she felt responsible for Alice. There was something she might have said or done that would have prevented the break, but what that was she had never discovered. She was almost reluctant to tell Richard that there had been a reconciliation.

"After all these years."

"She called and then came by. All of it quite out of the blue."

Richard frowned as she told him of Alice's visit with her male friend.

"Male friend?"

"Oh, I suppose they mean to marry. Or whatever substitute for it there is in their set."

"You can't mean you would approve of that!"

"Richard, no one asked my permission. Perhaps I am jumping to conclusions. I suppose a woman can have a male friend without any romantic overtones."

"Don't you believe it."

She turned away so as not to show her smile. Richard always came back to him and her.

"What is his name?"

"Oh, Richard, what difference does it make?"

But she told him finally, almost surprised that she remembered.

"Salvatore Bianco," he repeated. He might have been adding the name to a list in his mind.

14

Carl didn't realize the man was old until he came down to the sidewalk in response to his wave.

"You're Carl."

"Yes, sir."

"Mrs. Mortimer has told me about you."

"She's at St. Hilary's."

"I know that. My name is Professor Coburn. Mrs. Mortimer was also a professor, did you know that?"

Carl nodded.

"We were colleagues."

It seemed odd that the man would have called to him just to chat in this way, and Carl waited for the point of the conversation to be made clear. It turned out that Professor Coburn wanted to talk about Alice Mortimer.

"Has she been back to the house?"

Carl wasn't sure that he should talk about such things. Although the professor had mentioned his name, he was still a stranger. And an adult. Carl had learned that adults were very different and almost impossible to understand. Just when he thought he had the hang of them, he'd be surprised. This was true even of his mother. She was glad that he was so involved in computers, but when he told her of tapping into the police database and visiting Lieutenant Horvath at police headquarters, she went cold.

"I wish you wouldn't go there."

"I just went once."

"Okay." She drew him to her and ran her fingers through his hair.

Carl just didn't get it. He was puzzled by Professor Coburn as well. It was funny that with Lieutenant Horvath he hadn't felt that way, as if he had to be always on his guard against some unexpected change in the atmosphere. It helped a bit to pretend that the professor was a policeman, too, and his questions meant to assure Mrs. Mortimer's safety.

"Mrs. Mortimer told me her daughter came back alone and spent time in the house."

"That's right." If Mrs. Mortimer had told him this, there seemed no reason not to talk about it.

"Mr. Bianco wasn't with her."

"No."

"You sound relieved. Did he frighten you?"

Carl tried to describe the man's eyes, but in the midst of it he noticed a similar cold look in Professor Coburn's eyes. He might have gone on and told him about Lieutenant Horvath, but he didn't. It wasn't anything the professor said, but Carl didn't want to stand here on the sidewalk, answering questions.

"I gotta get to work."

A smile took over the professor's face, and he was once again a nice old man. "Good boy. You must give a day's work for a day's pay."

"I get paid by the hour."

"An hour's work for an hour's pay, then." He reached

out, but Carl was turning away. He felt the old man's eyes on him as he trotted across the lawn to where he had left the mower. He finished the row and was coming back before he looked toward the street. Professor Coburn was getting into an automobile parked several doors away.

Later he went out to the garage to check the rack of storm windows. Mrs. Mortimer had mentioned the annual task of washing them before putting them up. The screens were then racked for the winter.

"I should get all-weather windows, I suppose, but it seems silly to put more money into the house."

Each window had its location etched on its side, cut in with a knife and then smoothed by the coat of paint that covered it. There was a ladder as well, with an extension to get to the second-story windows. Behind the rack was the cabinet, its door shut. Carl moved the storm windows a third of the way out of the rack as he had done before and crawled behind them. He eased the door open but could not see inside. He reached in, and his hand fell on the package he had put there.

After he had closed the cabinet and pushed the storm windows back in place, he came out of the garage and yelped when he saw Salvatore Bianco coming around the house. The big man turned and saw him and kept on coming toward him. The garage door was sliding down behind him. As if to erase all thought of the cabinet and the hidden envelope, Carl began to walk toward the big man, who stopped abruptly and waited for him.

"Alice here?"

"No."

Just then, from the house, came a voice. "Sal? I'm up here."

Alice's face was visible in an upstairs window, her cheek pressed against the screen as if to make herself more visible. The big man glared at Carl and turned toward the house.

Carl ran out of the yard and down the alley. A block away was a gas station that had a pay phone booth near the sidewalk. He dialed the number Lieutenant Horvath had given him, asked for him, and was put on hold. Music flooded his ear. He should have said it was an emergency. Two minutes went by before he heard the voice of Lieutenant Horvath.

"This is Carl Hospers. You told me to call you if Salvatore Bianco came back to Mrs. Mortimer's house. He's there now."

"Whare are you?"

"At a pay phone."

"Away from the house?"

"Yes."

"Don't go back."

The phone went dead, and Carl stepped out of the booth. His bike was at Mrs. Mortimer's, and he thought of going back down the alley and seeing if he could retrieve it without being seen; but he decided against it. Still, he didn't want to miss out on whatever Lieutenant Horvath intended to do.

In the trash behind the station was a large pasteboard carton. It was in such good shape, Carl felt almost guilty taking it, but it had obviously been thrown away. He held it above his head and went quickly up the alley. Before he got to Mrs. Mortimer's he stopped, got out his knife, and cut a window in one side of the box, near the bottom. Then he upended it and let it down slowly over his shoulders until he could look through the little window. A minute later the carton was in position near Mrs. Mortimer's trash can, with Carl inside. He had a good view of the house, but the police could come and go in the front and he would never know it. He thought of moving gradually across the lawn but decided against it. Anyone would notice a pasteboard carton that moved across the lawn all by itself.

15

When Cy Horvath discovered that Sal Bianco had a wife within the confines of St. Hilary's parish, he didn't know what to think. Maybe Keegan had gotten it wrong from Marie Murkin that Mrs. Mortimer had told Father Dowling that her daughter had brought her fiancé to see her and that the man was Sal Bianco. Even as he thought about that chain of secondhand sources, Cy doubted the information. But doubt did not put his mind at rest.

There was no doubt that Bianco had accompanied Alice Mortimer on the visit to her mother's. She would come to know men like Bianco, working where she did. What she would know about him would not make him a very likely boyfriend. So why would she ask him to come along?

What Cy thought of next was pure guesswork, and he would have been ashamed to express it out loud to Phil Keegan. Under Keegan, Fox River detectives were trained to keep their imaginations under control and be guided by ascertainable facts. The only facts in the present case were that Bianco had been brought to her mother's house by Alice, that Bianco had been questioned about the body found in the car in the Chicago River, and that Alice's reconciliation with her mother was interpreted to have something to do with her expectations as her mother's sole heir. To conclude from this that Alice Mortimer meant to employ a gorilla like Bianco to speed up her inheritance was completely unwarranted, wild guesswork, sheer imagination. So why did he think that this was what was going on?

Carl's telephone call telling him that Bianco had shown up was transferred to him in his car, and he was on his way to the Mortimer home immediately. He decided to come up the alley, where he was less likely to be noticed, and approach the house through the backyard.

He cut the motor and drifted to a stop behind the Mortimer garage, out of sight of the house. He got out of the car, easing the door shut, then looked around the corner of the garage before making the turn. Near the trash was a pasteboard carton. Horvath moved quickly to it and crouched behind it, his eyes on the house.

He could see a car in the driveway, slightly visible between a large lilac bush and the house. They must be inside. His plan was to surprise Bianco in the house and haul him in for breaking and entering, taking the daughter as well, making as big a stink about it as he could. Of course he'd have to let them go; there was no charge he could make stick, since Mrs. Mortimer was not likely to regard her daughter as an intruder. But taking them in for questioning would alert them that whatever they were up to, they were now under surveillance. Cy figured he wouldn't have to say a thing to Keegan to justify the arrest, and the net effect would be to make any attempt on Mrs. Mortimer's life unlikely. Salvatore Bianco was not going to try anything if the police might be watching from behind any tree. Or pasteboard box.

There was stirring inside the carton. Cy edged back, still in a crouch. Was some animal trapped in there? He reached out and slapped the side of the box. It began to tip toward the house, to rock, and then it fell over. There was a kid inside!

Cy scrambled to his feet, feeling foolish, as if he were out in the backyard playing hide-and-seek with the kids. And then he saw Carl Hospers crawling out of the box.

"I was keeping an eye on the house," Carl said, emerging on hands and knees.

From the driveway came the sound of a car starting. Horvath, gun in hand now, leapt over the pasteboard carton and loped across the yard, but by the time he went between the house and lilac bush, the car had hit the street, changed gears, and was on its way. Sal Bianco was at the wheel, and he was alone. The side door opened and a sassy-looking woman stood there.

"What the hell are you doing?"

"Police. Are you Alice Mortimer?"

"Police! I didn't call the police."

"That was Salvatore Bianco who just drove away, ma'am."

Her expression changed. "Who?"

"I'm not surprised you don't know him. This is not his kind of neighborhood."

"What's that supposed to mean?"

"How many men do you know who have the police following them around?"

Cy realized that Carl had come to stand beside him. "This your son, ma'am?"

Alice Mortimer didn't know what to say to the different roles he was casting her for. Housewife who had no idea there were goons like Bianco in the world, mother of a son.

"You finish your work, Carl?" she asked the boy.

Carl didn't like the suggestion that he was working for her. Another car had turned in and was coming up the driveway. Cy put his gun away. Mrs. Mortimer got out of the passenger side of the car, and a large older man got out from behind the wheel. Mrs. Mortimer looked from her daughter to Cy and then to Carl, unable to know what to make of this welcoming party. The old man who had been driving came right up to Cy, a stern look on his face.

"Are you Salvatore Bianco?"

Alice's laughter saved the situation, though Cy didn't like the derisive implications of it. Mrs. Mortimer was assuring her companion that this was no Bianco. Cy, feeling not a little foolish, got out his ID and displayed it.

"We got a call that there was a suspicious character in the neighborhood."

"Alice!"

"No, a man."

"Bianco," the old man blurted out.

Cy said nothing. He saluted and went across the lawn and out to the alley.

"I'm sorry, Lieutenant." Carl had come along with him.

"What for? Who knows what might have happened if you hadn't made that call?"

He punched Carl lightly on the arm and got behind the wheel. "Can I drop you somewhere?"

"I've got my bike."

"So long."

He saluted again. He felt as if he were escaping. What would Captain Keegan make of this when he heard of it, as he surely would? But the best defense was a good offense. Cy headed toward the Loop.

The Cat Nap Lounge was dimly lit and, in the late afternoon, between the daytime drinkers and the desperate souls who sought amusement in such dives after the sun went down, was all but deserted. Cy took a stool at the bar, and almost immediately a girl sat down beside him. The bartender approached, trying to catch the girl's eye—he would recognize a cop at once—but she asked in a wheedling voice if he'd like to buy a girl a drink.

"Ice water," Cy said. "And one for my friend."

"Ice water?" the girl gurgled.

"It's good for you. Do you know Alice Mortimer?"

"Is that her last name?"

"What precinct you with, Officer?" the bartender said in a warning voice.

"Two ice waters," Cy repeated, and the bartender left them.

"How do you know Alice?"

"You got a brother?" he asked her.

She pushed back and looked at him. After a moment she nodded. "I guess you could be her brother."

"I know you don't want to talk about it and the bartender will give you trouble if you do, so answer me just one question quick. Were Alice and Sal going together a year ago?"

Her rounded eyes drifted to the bartender. She nodded twice, then looked to see if he got it and slid off her stool.

"Enjoy your ice water, polar bear."

The bartender put two glasses of ice water on the bar in

front of Cy and stared at the disappearing girl.

"She coming back?"

"The other's for you," Cy said, picking up one glass and nodding at the other. The bartender tried to grin, then gave it up. His hand went out for the glass and gripped it.

"To law and order," Cy said, lifting his.

"Yeah."

They clinked glasses, and the bartender took a quick sip and then sidled down the bar. Cy drank as if from real thirst and then walked slowly out of the Cat Nap.

Since he was in for a penny, he might just as well be in for a pound. Conjecturing that Alice and Bianco were conspiring to hasten her mother's death naturally took his mind back to the death of the father. He headed his car back to the west and Fox River.

A note on his desk told him that Carl Hospers had called. Remembering the fiasco in the backyard of the Mortimer house, Cy smiled. What a kid! Hiding in that carton had been a great idea until he'd come along and spoiled it. What struck him was that Carl hadn't panicked when the carton tipped and tumbled him out of it. Or had he known that it was Cy Horvath who had taken cover behind his hiding place? He picked up the phone and punched out the number. The line was busy.

When he looked it up, Harry Mortimer's obituary listed no present place of employment. Of course the man was of retirement age, but there was no mention of where he had worked, either. He had served in Korea, and the VFW had provided an honor guard. Maybe that was a place to start.

16

Tuttle enlisted Peanuts's help, but he decided he had better not be completely frank about what they were doing. Peanuts was no quiz kid, and in the battle of cops and robbers his allegiance was equivocal, given the reputation his family had acquired—rightly or wrongly, Tuttle added in case anyone was reading his mind—over the years in Fox River. The theory that Peanuts was the family's eyes and ears on the force, a Trojan horse keeping them informed, wouldn't wash with anyone who knew Peanuts. But one thing he was was loyal to his family, and Tuttle had long since learned to steer very clear of any questions bearing on the activities of the Pianones. Or any activities that might just barely impinge on those of the Pianones. It seemed best not to make it clear that they were on a trail that involved Salvatore Bianco.

Bianco was a hit man, Tuttle had no doubt of that, though he would have been able to deny under oath that he had any certain knowledge to that effect.

"What you want to do in a place like this?" Peanuts asked when Tuttle parked behind the place in Cicero.

"This is where Harry Mortimer hung out when he wasn't at Arlington or on a quick trip to Vegas."

Peanuts took the lie in without visible effect. Maybe he didn't remember who Mortimer was. Well, he could imagine he was a client. In a way, Tuttle hoped he was. His daughter almost had been.

The questions Alice Mortimer had put to him stayed in Tuttle's mind. A lawyer became used to the impatience of relatives expecting to inherit something. What might come seemed already owned and unjustly possessed by the bequeathing relative. Resentment rather than gratitude was the dominant feeling. Not that Tuttle condemned this desire to get what one felt was owed. He would like to get a piece of whatever Alice Mortimer was expecting. The trouble still was that there didn't seem much of a pie to slice up—or even taken as a whole, since Alice wouldn't have to share whatever her mother left with any other relative, there being none.

He might have forgotten about it, since she never came back to him, except that from things Peanuts said, he gathered interest was being shown in Mrs. Mortimer at headquarters. Of course, she was a fairly frequent visitor to the St. Hilary Parish Center, and Father Dowling and Captain Keegan had been friends since boyhood, so maybe it meant something and maybe it didn't. Tuttle had heard about Richard Coburn's renewed interest in Mrs. Mortimer, picking this up from Wexford, a member of the security force on the campus where Mrs. Mortimer and Coburn had taught.

"They were just friends until the husband died, and then he had an open track, or thought he did, but she gave him the cold shoulder."

Behind Wexford in his glassed-in office off the main lobby of the college administration building, a miniature

TV set was tuned to a soap opera. Apparently Wexford's duties did not interfere with his entertainment. His account of Coburn and Mrs. Mortimer sounded suspiciously like the plot of the television fare Wexford filled his head with.

"That pretty general knowledge?"

Wexford dipped his head and looked wise. "I doubt most people around here had any idea."

"But you did?"

"Molly," Wexford said.

"Molly?"

"Departmental secretary at the time. Tuttle, what a departmental secretary doesn't know isn't worth knowing. He tried to make a move on her while her husband was still alive."

"Yeah?"

"Coburn was a persistent guy, according to Molly, and if persistence was all it took, he would have been successful. But Professor Mortimer was not that kind of lady."

"You knew her."

"Listen, Tuttle, I've worked here how long, sitting here on display, and how many members of the faculty even notice me sitting here, let alone say hello? Don't ask. The answer is depressing. I'm an ornament. See that ceiling light? They notice that as much as they do me. Well, Mrs. Mortimer never failed to stop by and say a word or two. And not condescending, I don't mean that, she just noticed other people. And she was good with her students, even the nutty ones."

"Nutty in what way?"

"Take Gobel. A middle-aged guy, comes back to school after a military career, he gets a crush on her."

"Like Coburn?"

"Worse. Once he locked himself in her office, she's in there, too, and read long passages from Robert Browning to her and wouldn't let her go until he finished. The idea was that the poet said it so much better than he could and he wanted her to hear it as if he had written it. Nuts." But Wexford smiled wistfully.

"What happened?"

"After they took him away? I never heard."

"Coburn ever lock her in an office?"

Wexford laughed. "You'd have to know him to know how funny that is."

"How so?"

"Dignified." Wexford sat up on his chair and puffed out his chest and rolled out his lower lip. "Molly said it must have killed him when Professor Mortimer turned him down."

"Before she was a widow."

"It didn't matter. Coburn thought he had an open track once Mortimer was gone, but nothing had changed. She actually had a date with Willard Hanson, Willy, we all called him. That flattened Coburn. He sat in his office and got drunk, spent the night there. He was seated there sound asleep when Molly came in the morning, his whiskers sprouting out of those fat cheeks, eyes red. And all he said was 'Good morning,' as if everything were as usual. Molly didn't dare say anything to the contrary."

"Willard Hanson still around?"

Wexford's eyes rolled upward toward the neglected ceiling light. "The poor man was dead within a week. Found dead in the parking lot. Slipped and fell on the ice and wasn't found until the next day, dead as a mackerel."

"Drunk?"

"Willy? Never!"

The coroner had found no alcohol in the blood. The cause of death was exposure to cold, with the wound on the back of the head mentioned but not causally related, since he had crawled after having slipped and banged his head on the ice.

"You know her husband at all?"

Wexford hunched forward and rolled his chair closer to Tuttle. "How she ever married a guy like that I'll never know. Oh, I liked him. He was a real tout, always had a horse for you. A real loser. Until the end."

"What do you mean?"

"The rumor was he hit a huge number on a bet just days before he died."

"What did he die of?"

"Happiness?"

Because of the money? "How much?"

Wexford put his hands together and then drew them apart. He kept increasing the distance between them. He looked like a fisherman telling of a prize catch.

"That much?"

"It was the big enchilada, Tuttle."

It sounded like enough to retire on, if Mortimer had been so inclined. Wexford dismissed the suggestion that Mortimer could have gambled it away in the time between his win and his death. So where had all that money gone? Presumably to his widow. Add that to what Mrs. Mortimer ostensibly had, and Alice's interest made more sense. And so did Sal Bianco's. She might think he was interested in helping her get that money, but it was more likely that he would like to return it to the people from whom Mortimer had won it.

"You're sure he didn't lose it? Easy come, easy go?"

"Believe me, Tuttle, not even he could have done that." Wexford looked to the right and left, although there were only the two of them in the little office. He lowered his voice. "Lucky for Professor Mortimer he died when he did." He crossed himself quickly, as if to unsay what he had said.

That was the thought Tuttle took back to his office with him. He was preoccupied when Peanuts came by with an anchovy pizza and a six-pack of soda.

"You're busy I'll come another time." Peanuts was mad that his surprise had not had an effect.

"Good Lord, no, Peanuts. I was just thinking of a case. Sit down, sit down. Mmmm, does that smell good."

Placated, Peanuts popped open the box and handed Tuttle a hot, dripping slice of pizza. His own mouth was full when he next spoke. Tuttle realized that Peanuts was asking what case had been bothering him.

"And spoil this treat? Forget it, it doesn't matter."

But Peanuts insisted he tell him. Tuttle sometimes admitted to himself that Peanuts was the best friend he had. He supposed he was Peanut's best friend, too, and the little cop didn't want to run the risk of disturbing things. So he told him about Harry Mortimer making the win of his lifetime just before he died.

Peanuts shook his head. "He die of natural causes?"

"You could find that out easier than I could."

Peanuts nodded, making a little circle of his thumb and index finger. "Done."

17

Marie Murkin was on the lookout for Sylvia Bianco, no matter the teasing way Father Dowling had brought up the woman's attendance at St. Hilary's. Even when she said she hadn't seen such a person, the image of a timid little lady who ducked into a back pew, always coming late, always leaving early, came to her. Could that be Mrs. Bianco?

The following Saturday afternoon, at the five o'clock mass that fulfilled the Sunday obligation, Marie was in the choir loft, where she had a nice view of the whole church, when the woman slipped into a pew just below her. Not taking any chances, Marie descended to the church level and took up her station in the vestibule. As soon as communion began to be distributed, the woman pushed through the doors and into the vestibule.

"Give me a hand, would you, dear?" Marie called out, having turned toward the pamphlet rack and filled her arms with literature. She held her breath, wondering if the woman would respond, and then she was aware of her at her elbow. "Just put these in the rack."

She transferred the pamphlets to the little woman, effectively pinning her to the spot.

"Thank you, thank you. That's nice."

She went outside with the woman after the pamphlets were back in place and on the steps put out her hand. "I'm Marie Murkin."

"How do you do." She let Marie take her hand, but her eyes slipped toward the parking lot.

"I'll walk you to your car, if you'd like. There's something I want to ask you."

"What?"

Marie laughed and put her hand on the little woman's arm. "Don't be alarmed. I only need you for an hour or two. Are you free Monday afternoon?"

"Monday?"

"Come about one-thirty. We'll do the Blessed Mother's altar first."

Marie could see the woman's opposition crumble. How could she refuse a request like that? The car she led them to was a massive black limousine. It was almost comic to see the tiny woman slip behind the wheel.

"Monday at one-thirty," Marie called.

Mrs. Bianco nodded as the huge car began to creep toward the street. Marie Murkin turned and went humming toward the rectory. As she passed the church, the doors opened and the congregation began to pour out. She had to skip and half run to get out of the way. Honestly. But of course that was the trouble with this Saturday evening mass. People went just to get it out of the way so they could spend all day Sunday in front of their television sets. But the annoyance did not remove Marie's sense of having accomplished much. She was still humming when Father Dowling came back.

"Supper in half an hour," she sang out.

"Phil Keegan's coming."

"You might have told me."

"I thought I had. I could call and tell him not to come. He could stop at McDonald's, I suppose."

It was best to ignore it when he started to tease. "Gerry is having dinner with the Hosperses, so there'll be plenty. By the way, I spoke with Mrs. Bianco after mass."

"Was she there?"

"I asked her to help me with the altar on Monday afternoon."

"Good. Good."

Marie would have liked to tell how she had managed to corner the woman and persuade her to come, but the pastor was annoyingly disinterested. In her kitchen, mumbling to herself, Marie felt deflated. Why did she expect Father Dowling to regard her speaking to a parishioner as an accomplishment? With some reluctance she pushed the subject from her mind and concentrated on the meal she was preparing.

But when the pastor and Phil Keegan had finished and she was pouring their coffee, Father Dowling brought it up.

"Marie has struck up an acquaintance with Salvatore Bianco's wife."

"His first wife?"

"Is there more than one?" Marie was so shocked, she pulled out a chair and sat.

"So far. He seems pretty close to Alice Mortimer."

Marie clamped a hand over her mouth, but not before an anguished cry escaped. What a dreadful thing. This would kill old Mrs. Mortimer. And what would happen to the mousy little woman who had promised to come on Monday afternoon to help decorate Mary's altar?

"You think he's serious about Alice, Phil?"

"I don't think one thing or another beyond what I'm told. Cy thinks it might be a business relationship."

"What kind of business?"

"Monkey business." Phil laughed as if he had surprised himself with that answer. "Well, he is a gorilla."

"What kind of monkey business?" Marie asked. She could strangle Phil Keegan for making a joke of this. Surely he must know what a wonderful old lady Mrs. Mortimer was. Thank God she had the friendship of the man she had brought to the rectory. Professor Coburn. It was odd to think that Liz was Professor Mortimer.

"Oh, it's just some speculation on Cy's part. The daughter and Bianco have been to the house several times. Looking for something they haven't found, probably because it isn't there."

"What?"

Phil shrugged. "Look, I'm sorry I said anything. It's not the policy of the department to sit around dreaming up things. Cy Horvath was very reluctant to tell me what his idea was. No wonder."

"But those two were at the house when Liz was here at the center?"

"I guess so."

Marie shook her head. "I think you should let Edna know this, Father. It doesn't seem right to let Carl work there if people are going to be breaking into the house looking for God knows what."

Phil threw up his arms. "Why don't I keep my big mouth shut?"

"Is that a rhetorical question?" Father Dowling asked.

But he could say things like that to Phil Keegan, the

two of them being such old friends. The pastor stood and Phil Keegan followed suit, and they went off to the study, after telling Marie what a fine meal it had been.

"You haven't had dessert!"

Phil stopped in the doorway. "What is it?"

"Lemon meringue pie."

"Serve it in the study, will you, Marie?" Father Dowling called from the hallway.

"Do you need any help?" Phil Keegan asked.

"Run along with Father. I'll bring it to you."

Men were boys after all, Marie decided. Mention a piece of lemon meringue pie, and a big gruff detective like Phil Keegan was suddenly twelve years old. The pie was missing the piece Gerry had had before leaving for the Hosperses'.

She served their dessert in the study and ten minutes later took the dishes away, closing the study door after her. The way the two of them smoked, it was a wonder they didn't set off the smoke alarms.

Dishes done, Marie went up the back stairs to her room, where she settled down. Before she turned on her television set, she sat for a moment, staring across the room, thinking of that frightened little woman, Mrs. Bianco. What did Lieutenant Horvath imagine her husband was up to with Alice Mortimer? For half an hour Marie tried to hit upon some way she could find out, but in the end she gave up. Besides, her program was now on.

18

Father Dowling found that Phil Keegan was not at all reluctant to speculate about Salvatore Bianco and other matters in the privacy of the rectory study, with the Cubs on and a good cigar going. With the slightest of prompting, Phil laid out the suspicions of his department as well as the present state of their knowledge. It was best to just let Phil talk when the mood was on him, and Father Dowling did not interrupt, saying only enough to keep the narrative going. Only afterward, when Phil had left, did he sort out what Phil had said.

1. Alice Mortimer, now calling herself Alice Morton, the more or less wayward daughter of Liz Mortimer, had suddenly shown up at the house in the company of a man the mother assumed was at least her daughter's boyfriend and perhaps her fiancé.

2. The man was Salvatore Bianco, who
   a. was already married,
   b. was known to the police as an unsavory character, probably guilty of many crimes for which he would never pay, and

c. had been routinely brought in for questioning when the body of Eugene Welsheim, a welshing gambler, was found in the Chicago River.

3. This background suggested that Alice's unexpected reunion with her mother, in company with Bianco, might very well pose a threat to Mrs. Mortimer, because

   a. Alice was her only heir, and

   b. there was some reason to think that Harry Mortimer had won a large amount of money prior to his death, thus making Alice's inheritance far more interesting than it would otherwise be.

4. Salvatore Bianco, given his associations, was likely to know about such gambling winnings.

5. It was difficult not to speculate about Harry Mortimer's death: had it indeed been an accident?

"But didn't he die of a heart attack, Phil?" Father Dowling had asked.

"Who?"

"Mr. Mortimer."

"There may have been a heart attack involved."

"What do you say he died of?"

"Breathing."

Father Dowling waited because of the little smile on Phil's face.

"Breathing when he was sitting behind the wheel of his automobile with the motor running while parked in the garage with the door shut."

* * *

In the privacy of his own study, Father Dowling was equally willing to formulate what Cy Horvath seemed to suspect. It was this.

Harry Mortimer, a lifetime gambler and legendary loser, won a massive sum of money and a few days later was found dead, presumably having had a heart attack just after pulling his car into the garage and thus rendered incapable of turning off the motor. What Cy obviously thought happened was that irate gamblers, stung by the great loss Mortimer's win represented and angry when he did not immediately resume betting as he always had before, threatened him unsuccessfully and then brought about his death. How to get the money now?

The weak point of the theory was the long delay between the death of Harry Mortimer and the next stage. On the assumption that his widow had possession of the money, Sal Bianco struck up a friendship with Alice Mortimer so that, when Mrs. Mortimer died, her death hastened by Bianco, he could lay his money on Mr. Mortimer's winnings and restore it to his bosses.

Father Dowling smiled. No wonder Phil was impatient with Cy's theory, even when it was implied and not stated. Spelled out as he had just done, it seemed fantasy indeed. There were too many logical jumps. For example, if Mortimer's death had been accidental, as it was judged to be at the time, an important prop was removed by the theory. Still, the theory was not mortally wounded. The gambling bosses, hearing of Mortimer's death and realizing he had recently won a large sum of their money, which he had not reinvested in any casino or at any track, would understandably dream of getting their hands on his stash. But was there indeed sufficient evidence that Harry Mortimer had won a large sum of money? Take that away, and the theory collapsed. There was one way to find that out, and, emptying his pipe and turning off his Mr. Coffee preparatory to retiring for the night, Father Dowling resolved to settle that question as soon as possible.

"Did you notice Mrs. Mortimer at mass?" he asked Marie when he settled down to his Sunday dinner the following day.

"Notice her?"

"Was she there?"

Marie inhaled and let her eyes drift toward the ceiling. "When I do manage to waylay a parishioner on their way out of church, I am subjected to such mocking that—"

"Marie, I'm sorry. I always give you credit for a sense of humor you obviously do not have."

"Is that supposed to be an apology?"

"It is meant to be commensurate with my offense."

She thought about it and then apparently decided not to waste time on picky details. "She came to the ten."

"Thank you."

"Well, why did you want to know?"

"Just curious."

"But why? There were lots of other people there. Do you want me to mention them?"

"If you'd like."

Even as he teased Marie, Father Dowling felt bad about it, but try as he would, he could not resist the opportunity when it arose. Marie readily cast herself in the role of his assistant—if not vice versa—so that any failure to exclude her from what she regarded as parish business offended her. That meant he sometimes innocently caused her offense—obviously there were limits to what he might confide to her—but what he was doing now was extra.

"Marie, I want to talk with Liz, and I'd rather not wait until tomorrow. I might drop by her house later."

"Should I call and see if she's there?"

He resisted the opportunity to annoy her. "Thank you. Ask when it would be convenient for me to come."

Left alone, he turned over a few pages of the newspaper, then set it aside. He tried not to read at meals. His food went cold and he wasted too much time at table when he did.

"Two o'clock will be fine," Marie said cheerily when she returned. "I told her we'd be there then."

"We!"

"She specifically asked me to come along."

"At your suggestion?"

Marie lifted her chin and marched into the kitchen. Father Dowling had been checkmated and he knew it. However Marie had wangled an invitation, if Liz had indeed asked her, there was no way he could withdraw the invitation. Of course, he could decide not to go himself. But that would be to postpone until Monday discovering whether or not Harry Mortimer had won a large sum of money just prior to his death.

19

Liz Mortimer had been delighted to receive the call from the rectory asking if Father Dowling could come by and see her this afternoon.

"Why don't you come, too, Mrs. Murkin?"

"Oh, I don't think so. Father Dowling asked—"

"But I'm inviting you."

"Mrs. Mortimer, I don't make calls with the pastor. If you want to talk with me, I could come some other time or you could stop by here."

"But mine is a social invitation. Professor Coburn will also be here."

That removed Marie Murkin's reluctance, which had not sounded insuperable in any case. Mrs. Mortimer had noticed the housekeeper's interest in Richard when she had brought him to meet Father Dowling. Liz Mortimer still did not know what to do about Richard Coburn. He was an imposing figure of a man, he obviously had his health, and despite having moved to a condo in a retirement complex, he certainly was in no way disposed to think of his life as over. He had spoken to Liz in what could only be taken as a proposal of marriage, and while she had managed to deflect discussion from it at the time, she knew she could not go on pretending she didn't understand what he was saying. What answer would she give him when the question was put to her unequivocally?

Richard's interst in her when Harry had still been alive had been easy to repel. What kind of woman did he think she was? She had put that question to him the other day when he'd advanced what sounded like a proposal.

"The kind who would repel such an advance," he said complacently.

"And yet you made it."

"I wanted you to know how I feel about you."

"What difference could that make to a married woman?"

"Wives become widows. As indeed you have."

This was flattering, of course, just as his advances when Harry was still alive had not failed to stir her. Life with Harry had been such a trial, not just a matter of bad times that would give way to good times, but a perpetual and unchanging bad time. But her marriage had been a life sentence she intended to serve, making the best of it she could. Her husband had become an addicted gambler, her only child had become estranged, but she had her teaching and she had the house. In a moment of lucid contriteness, Harry had insisted that the house be held in her name alone.

"Do you know the expression 'bet the house,' Liz?"

"I get the idea, Harry."

Her eyes had filled with tears at this reminder of the better self that had once been his. He had harmed her so much by his gambling, but he wanted to insure that he could not deprive her utterly of what they had once had together. What hope and joy had been theirs when they'd bought the house! Harry had been in that same mood the last time they'd talked, just the day before he'd died. He had held her tightly and tried to tell her he was sorry for all the anguish he had caused her. That was when he'd pressed the little cardboard envelope into her hand.

"Hide this. Bury this. Never give it back to me or tell me where it is."

"What is it?"

He'd covered her lips with his fingers and shaken his head. "Hide it," he'd repeated in an urgent whisper.

When his body was found in the garage behind the wheel of his car, Liz had driven far from her thoughts that he had committed suicide, seizing on the suggestion that he had suffered a heart attack and been unable to turn off the motor. Thank God the coroner had not thought to wonder how the garage door had come to be closed.

She had also forgotten all about the envelope he had given her until long after the shock of his death had subsided. Whatever the little red envelope contained did not interest her. It seemed a symbol of Harry's final wish to change his life. He had not lived long enough to do that. She had actually forgotten the red envelope, and when she'd come upon it one day in the back of a dresser drawer, after Alice had surprised her with a telephone call, she had given it to Carl and told him to put it in the garage.

"Where?"

She'd thought wildly for a moment and then remembered the cabinet behind the window rack. Carl had gone off to the garage and she'd watched him go and again her eyes had filled with tears. It was like burying Harry a second time.

Now Richard Coburn's intentions were no longer ambiguous. On Saturday a letter from Richard had arrived by special messenger. It contained a formal proposal of marriage. There followed a declaration of his affection and esteem and the provisions of the proposed union. He would make her his sole heir and was prepared to lay before her the extent of his investments and savings. He thought they might pleasantly surprise her. He would sell his condo, and he supposed she would want to do the same with the house she had shared with Harry. A fresh start would be best.

Liz had read the letter several times. She was oddly disappointed. It seemed as much the proposal of a business merger as of marriage. She tried to counter this first reaction by reminding herself of their ages. It was unrealistic to expect Richard to be passionately emotional, and because of their experience with life, it made sense to attend to practical details. The letter was so rational that Liz scarcely knew what tack to take in reacting to it. She still did not know. A P.S. informed her that he would call on her Sunday afternoon. No wonder she welcomed the idea that Father Dowling wanted to come by. Inviting Marie Murkin provided further protection. At the very least, she wished to postpone any discussion of Richard's letter.

20

Tuttle spent several of the wee hours of Sunday morning in the Cat Nap. If the drinks hadn't been so watered, he might have been drunk when he went out to his car for the nap that, despite its name, he was unlikely to get inside the lounge, where music of a kind Tuttle hated was played so loudly that the fillings in his teeth tingled. He settled behind the wheel of his car and tipped his trusty tweed hat over his eyes and waited for sleep to come.

It didn't. Inside he hadn't been able to stop yawning. It was hours past his normal bedtime. Now he feared he was getting a second wind. Alice was on a shift that went until two A.M., another twenty minutes, so it was probably just as well that he couldn't sleep. The main reason he was keeping an eye on her was to alert Peanuts in case she unexpectedly left work early. Peanuts was going through her apartment. Tuttle just hoped that her refrigerator didn't prove tempting.

He fell asleep. When he awoke only a few cars were still parked around him. It took him a while to get his watch into light enough to read the dial. Yipes! It was going on four in the morning. He had the motor started and roared out of the lot before he knew where he was going. Alice's shift was long over, and Peanuts should have gotten out of her place long before she got home. The original plan was to meet at Tuttle's office, where the lawyer would debrief Peanuts and find out what the search of Alice's apartment had yielded. He thought of Peanuts showing up at his office and not finding him there. How long would he have waited? Just on a hunch, Tuttle thought he would check.

Peanuts sat on the hallway floor, his back against Tuttle's office door, his head tilted forward, sound asleep. Tuttle shook him awake.

"Wanna get something to eat, Peanuts?"

"What time is it?"

"Breakfast time."

"Where you been?"

"I fell asleep."

"Me too."

That seemed to even it off as far as Peanuts was concerned, and that got Tuttle off the hook.

They drove to a twenty-four-hour diner, where they ordered waffles, bacon and eggs, and eight-ounce glasses of juice. For twenty minutes there was only the happy sound of feeding, with some country-western in the background.

"What did you find out, Peanuts?"

"Nothing."

"Nothing at all?"

"I didn't get in."

"What?"

"There was a dog next door."

Peanuts was afraid of dogs. Tuttle knew this, and one

of the foundations of their friendship was that he did not give Peanuts a hard time about it. When Peanuts was a kid and walked half a mile to school every day, he had two choices of route, and that came down to a choice between two dogs that lay in wait for him and barked him on his way, nipping at his heels.

"That's why I quit school."

"Grade school?"

"I got my high school diploma," Peanuts had said indignantly. Was he trying to explain why he hadn't gone to college?

A dog next door to Alice's place would have immobilized Peanuts, Tuttle understood that. Somehow he couldn't get angry about it, not even when he thought of the dead hours he had spent in the Cat Nap and sleeping in his car outside.

"Probably nothing there anyway," he said magnanimously.

"I never did know what I was supposed to look for."

Neither did Tuttle. Peanuts might be afraid of dogs, but Tuttle had learned that the little cop was lucky, too.

"Wanna go take a look at her place?"

Tuttle lifted his bewhiskered face to the clock on the wall. "What for? It'll be light in an hour."

"That's what I mean."

Tuttle looked into Peanut's narrowed eyes. The expression seemed meant to suggest shrewdness.

"We'll go by there when you drop me at my place."

They were using the squad car that Peanuts had borrowed for his night's surveillance. It provided good cover.

"The lights are on," Peanuts said when they parked

across the street from the house in which Alice had one of four apartments. Lights were on in the upper-right-hand corner.

"I told you. She's home."

"Come on." Peanuts pushed open the door of the car and crossed the street. Tuttle hurried after him. From behind a fence came the warning snarl of a dog. Peanuts took Tuttle's arm and quickened his pace. Tuttle felt he was being arrested. It must have been fear of that dog that made Peanuts head for the front door and pull. It opened. He flitted inside, Tuttle right behind him.

"Now what?"

Peanuts just started up the stairs. On the landing he said, "I'm a cop."

A moment later he was banging on the door. He whispered to Tuttle, "I'll pretend she called the police."

Good idea. But half a minute went by and no one came to the door. Tuttle tried the knob. It turned. He pushed and the door opened. They entered side by side.

"Police," Peanuts called out.

She was in the bedroom, on the floor, staring at the ceiling with wide unseeing eyes.

"Yipes!" Peanuts cried.

"She's dead."

"I see that. Let's get out of here."

Another good idea. After he closed the door, Tuttle wiped the knob carefully. They walked and did not run across the street to the patrol car.

"You knew she was up there dead," Tuttle said.

"No." Just that, but Peanuts's stunned look underwrote the truth of what he said. He picked up the microphone, but Tuttle grabbed it from him.

"Wait. You call in from the car, you're involved. Why should we report it, Peanuts? Think. She's beyond help. We have to cover our tracks. Remember, I was hanging around the Cat Nap most of the night, and plenty of people will have noticed this patrol car. Where were you parked?"

"Parked? I never parked. Every time I tried to, that dog started in. I spent most of the night at your office."

"With me."

Peanuts started to shake his head, but then a light of low wattage came on in his eyes, and he nodded.

"I got it."

So had Alice Mortimer, Tuttle reflected, and it didn't make any sense at all.

21

After mass at a church his wife called St. Ethnics, Cy and Lydia Horvath had a quick breakfast and then played tennis until noon. Ageeably exhausted, they were then ready for a day of rest. His wife sacked out with a paperback novel, and Cy descended to the den he had built in the basement, uncapped a beer, and settled down for an afternoon of televised baseball. He was nodding before the first inning was over, and when the ringing telephone brought him wildly awake, it was time for the seventh inning stretch.

"Cy? Keegan. You been wondering about the Mortimers and their daughter and all that?"

"Yeah?"

"She just turned up dead."

"Aw. What was it, heart attack?"

"The daughter, not the old lady. Someone throttled her, Cy. Look, I know it's Sunday . . ."

"You downtown?"

"I'll come by for you. Five minutes?"

"Right."

Cy looked in at his wife, who was sound asleep. He scribbled a note and left it on the kitchen table and looked out to see Keegan turn in the drive. The captain must already have been in the neighborhood when he called.

"Where was she found?" Cy asked, getting into the car.

"Where she lives. Which is outside our territory. I made a call, indicating our interest, and we're welcome."

Borrowing trouble? As if they didn't have enough trouble in Fox River. But Cy knew all this was Keegan's vote of confidence in him. It was a way of accepting the validity of the questions he had been putting about Mrs. Mortimer and her daughter and her pal Bianco. Only this kicked his ideas in the head. He said as much to Keegan.

"Maybe Bianco figured he didn't need her."

Cy thought about it as Keegan roared along at sixty-five, weaving in and out of lanes like a commuter late for work.

"Cubs lost the first game," Keegan said.

"Yeah?"

They were getting ready to take the body away when they got there, but Chisholm, the man in charge, told them to wait a minute.

"You know her, Keegan?"

Cy shook his head. "I know who she is. Her mother lives in Fox River."

"You think the mother did this?" Chisholm was serious.

Cy said he didn't think so.

"What's your interest?"

Keegan looked at Cy, indicating he should spill it. "The daughter's been hanging around with Salvatore Bianco."

Chisholm's whistle sounded like a tire going flat. He glanced at the body. "So maybe he did it?"

"I suppose you'll want to put that question to him."

Chisholm smiled grimly.

"He lives in Fox River," Cy said. "We'll bring him in."

Chisholm liked it even better now that they were on a two-way street. "But I don't envy you. You better watch out for that guy."

"If we find him at home, things should go smoothly."

Cy's fingers started to cross, but he stopped them. On the way back to Fox River, Phil called in and asked for patrol car assistance in the arrest.

"Roger," said an all-too-recognizable voice.

"Is that you, Peanuts?"

"Closing on destination. Over and out."

Keegan tried in vain to raise Peanuts again.

"What's he doing in a patrol car on Sunday?" he demanded of Cy.

"Answering the radio."

Keegan increased the speed of the car. Obviously he did not want Peanuts getting to the scene first and giving Salvatore Bianco forewarning.

"If Bianco's there," Cy said.

Keegan slowed down. "You're right. Maybe. In any case, he'll have an alibi."

"Unless he was acting on his own."

"You're full of ideas lately."

The wrong ones. It was old Mrs. Mortimer he had thought might be in danger, not Alice. The only reason Bianco would have gotten rid of her—if all Cy's speculation made any sense—was that he had managed to lay his hands on Harry Mortimer's winnings and wanted to shut up the one who knew he had. But then Mrs. Mortimer would know. . . .

"Captain?"

Keegan glanced at him.

"We better have someone check on Mrs. Mortimer."

Phil began to nod before he finished. "Do it."

So Cy got on the radio and when Peanuts responded sent him to the Mortimer house.

"What am I looking for?"

"Just make sure everything's okay."

"Should I tell her about her daughter?"

"No. Call in when you get there."

"Roger."

Half a minute later Cy said, "How did he know about Alice Mortimer?"

Keegan's eyebrows lifted and his mouth turned down as he shrugged.

Mrs. Bianco, frightened half to death, said her husband was still in bed, and when Salvatore appeared his hair was tousled, his face puffy, his eyes still full of sleep.

"What?" He carefully tied the sash of his robe.

"Alice Mortimer is dead."

Sal glanced at his wife, then glared at Keegan. "Leave us alone," he barked at his wife. He closed the door after she left the room.

"What the hell right do you have to come into my house with that kind of garbage?"

"Garbage?"

"In front of my wife!" Bianco assumed a tone of injured righteousness.

"You know Alice Mortimer, right?"

"I know who she is." Bianco took a half-smoked cigar from a tray and put it in his mouth. The three of them still stood in the center of the living room. "I know where she works."

"You also know where her mother lives, don't you?" Keegan turned to Cy. "Check on Peanuts."

When Cy went into the kitchen to use the phone, Mrs. Bianco was huddled in the breakfast nook, her eyes as big as saucers.

"What has he done?"

"May I use your phone, Mrs. Bianco?"

His tone disarmed her. "Of course. of course."

"Got a directory?"

It took him a while to find the Mortimer number. He punched it out and waited. Finally it was answered.

"Mrs. Mortimer?"

"Yes."

He hung up. That was unforgivable, but he couldn't think of anything else to do. He certainly couldn't tell her what had happened to her daughter. That kind of message had to be delivered in person. Cruel as hanging up on her might be, it would have been far worse to tell her that her only child had been brutally murdered. The main thing was to know that she was all right. Her voice had conveyed no sense of concern. Peanuts would keep the house under surveillance until relieved.

"Who is Alice Mortimer?" Mrs. Bianco asked.

Cy couldn't hang up on her. "A young woman who was murdered earlier this morning. Your husband knew her."

"He was home at the time!"

"What time?"

"The time you said. This morning. He's been in bed asleep all night."

A wife can't testify against her husband, nor, as a practical matter, can she testify for him. Of course Mrs. Bianco would lie for her husband.

"Then he has nothing to worry about."

Mrs. Bianco looked as if she worried for a living. Cy went back to the living room with the sense that the satisfactions of police work did not outweigh its agonies.

Phil was seated in the center of the sofa, each hand gripping an arm of it, looking up at Bianco with a patient, incredulous expression.

"Mr. Bianco doesn't remember when he last saw Alice Mortimer. If he ever accompanied her to the home of her mother, it has slipped his memory. He has heard of the Cat Nap Lounge, but he can't recall if he ever visited the place."

"His wife said he was home all night, asleep."

"It's true." Bianco spoke as one who did not expect to be believed.

"I'd like to get your statement down in writing, Mr. Bianco. Could you accompany us downtown?" Phil made "Mr. Bianco" sound like an insult.

"I'll ask my lawyer."

"By all means."

They adjourned to the kitchen, where Bianco picked up the phone, thought for a moment, shook his head, and picked up the directory from the table where Cy had left it. Cy stood next to him as he turned to the T's. His finger traced down the column, paused, then lifted to punch out a number. He waited and waited, and then there was the audible message of an answering machine.

"That's Tuttle," Phil Keegan said.

"That's who he called," Cy replied.

"Come on, Bianco. In the car, I'll contact one of our men who will be able to locate your lawyer."

"Yeah?"

"Peanuts Pianone."

Cy raised Peanuts as Phil was pulling away from the curb. Bianco had pulled on some clothes and sat sullenly in back.

"Pianone," Peanuts responded on the radio.

"Captain Keegan wants you to get hold of Tuttle and ask him to come downtown."

And suddenly, incredibly, the voice of Tuttle was heard.

"How can I be of service, Captain?"

"Tell him we have a client for him," Keegan growled.

22

When Phil Keegan arrived at the Mortimer house, Father Dowling went out to the car as Phil emerged.

"Roger! Thank God you're here."

"Something's happened?"

Old Mrs. Mortimer would not have wanted to hear of her daughter's death in the stark version Phil Keegan gave him. Father Dowling himself had to make an effort not to wince. Death by violence lost its horror for those who had to deal with it professionally. Phil recoiled more from the prospect of informing next of kin than he did from the dreadful event itself.

"Murder?"

"She was killed."

The priest nodded when Phil told him they had already talked with Salvatore Bianco.

"I'll give you a minute to tell the old lady. How do you think she'll take it?"

Father Dowling didn't answer. In these matters predictions were pointless. Phil got back into the car and got on the radio. Father Dowling returned to the Mortimer house more slowly than he had come out to meet Phil.

The group in the living room made a tableau. Liz sat

in a corner of the couch, Professor Coburn stood behind it, one great hand resting on the back of the couch in such a way that he might have been touching Liz Mortimer's shoulder. Marie Murkin had pulled a chair toward the old lady, rippling a throw rug in the process, and leaned toward Liz as if in support. No one was speaking. It was as if they had fallen dumb when he'd entered and now awaited what would clearly be bad news.

"Alice," the old woman said, raising her eyes to his.

"Yes."

She searched his face. "Dead?"

He came and sat beside her and conveyed to her in gentler tones what Phil Keegan had told him.

"The police want to talk with you to get what help you can give them in discovering who did it. You've met Captain Keegan."

"No."

"Not now, Father," Coburn said, standing even more erect, if possible. "They must show some consideration."

But Liz ignored her defender. "What help can I be, Father? We had become strangers, Alice and I." She looked toward the fireplace as if she had never noticed it before. "They should talk to the man she brought here."

Suddenly Liz looked old. She sat back and gestured toward her purse. Coburn sprang forward, handed it to her, and then hurried to the kitchen for water. A minute later, having swallowed her pills, Liz revived. The memory of the man her daughter had brought home obviously had a powerful effect on her. But his name eluded her momentarily, and her expression fleetingly expressed the fear that her memory was no longer at her beck and call.

"Salvatore Bianco? They're questioning him."

"Was he responsible?"

"They think so."

"I can believe it. He was a cruel man." She stopped herself, shaking her head impatiently. "I have no right to accuse him."

"Shall I bring in Captain Keegan now?"

"Let me talk to him," Coburn said, coming importantly around the couch.

"Richard!" Liz said, and then to Father Dowling, " 'If it were done, when 'tis done, then 'twere well it were done quickly.' "

How like an old teacher to quote Shakespeare at such a time.

Father Dowling left Marie Murkin at the Mortimer house. It was more difficult getting free of Professor Coburn.

"This is an outrage, Father, badgering the woman that way at a time like this."

"It's their job."

"That's no excuse."

This was gallantry, Father Dowling supposed. Coburn seemed delighted to play the role of Liz's protector. Would the old woman be more or less susceptible to her old colleague's attention now that her daughter was dead? Throughout the painful period of estrangement, Liz had lived in the hope that she and Alice would be reconciled. Even living at a distance from one another, they were still related by that ineradicable link between mother and child. Eventually, Liz had always been sure, her prodigal daughter would come home and they would rejoice together. In the event, she'd brought with her a man Liz had instinctively disliked. Had Bianco killed Alice? The man had an alibi, but Phil Keegan dismissed that as insignificant.

"His wife vouches for him, Roger."

Meaning that any wife would lie for her husband in such circumstances? Maybe not, but the little he knew of Sylvia Bianco made it easy for Father Dowling to believe that in her case, at least, Phil was right. Out of fear alone, she would do what she could to protect her husband.

Instead of going directly back to St. Hilary's, he drove to the Bianco home. Blinds or drapes shut off all the windows from the outside world, the closed doors looked doubly locked, the house might have been unoccupied. Nonetheless, he rang the bell. Having come out of his way, he would at least go through the motions. He did not ring the bell twice, however; he had turned from the door and started back to his car when he heard the sound. The door was being unlocked. It opened slightly.

"Father Dowling?"

He retraced his steps to where Sylvia Bianco, remaining well out of sight of curious neighbors, waited to let him in. He had not expected her to be alone, if she were here at all. But she was, a frightened little woman alone in her house after the ordeal of the police coming and taking away her husband. Her eyes grew large as she recounted it. Again Father Dowling had the sense that it was the shame of the thing, knowledge that it would become a neighborhood topic of talk, rather than the sheer fact of her husband's having been arrested, that overwhelmed the little woman.

"Have you called relatives?"

"His family would already know."

Was she saying they would know Salvatore had killed Alice?

"How about your own family?"

She emitted a sad little laugh.

"You have none?"

"A brother in Bayonne. I wouldn't call him up to tell him this."

"The police think your husband killed that young woman."

She began to shake her head. "They said it happened this morning. He was here."

"I suppose they'll think you're just protecting him."

"He was here." She sounded almost disappointed.

Back at the rectory, he lay down for forty winks, but it was five 'clock when he awoke. From below wafted the aroma of a pork roast. Father Dowling lay on his back, staring at the ceiling. He said a prayer for the repose of the soul of Alice Mortimer. Tomorrow he would offer a mass for her. Would her mother bring her back to Fox River for burial? What a sad brief round her life seemed. By contrast, Liz's life was rich, not least because of the crosses she had had to bear—an unreliable husband, a wayward daughter. She might have blamed herself and thereby added a third defeat to theirs. Her agony had consisted of accepting and supporting Harry and Alice no matter what. Now Liz was all alone. Except, perhaps, for Richard Coburn.

Father Dowling got up and moved to a chair, where he picked up his breviary, but before opening it, he thought again of Coburn. He seemed to be a strong, determined man, certainly someone on whom Liz could lean, if she were a woman in need of leaning on someone. At their age, the lure of companionship would be strong. Doubtless Liz would put off Coburn now, in the wake of Alice's death, but equally doubtless Coburn would persevere. Perhaps his perseverance would be repaid.

"They have the same eyes."

Carl's arresting remark about Coburn's resemblance to Salvatore Bianco was difficult to forget, and Father Dowling realized that the thought of an autumn marriage between Liz Mortimer and Professor Coburn made him uneasy. He had never himself noticed the expression in Coburn's eyes on which Carl had commented. Still, he did not doubt what the boy had seen. Adults forgot how memorable their deeds and words, even expressions, were to the young. Carl had shown distrust, almost fear, of Coburn, and Father Dowling had difficulty not sharing it.

He shook his head. What a busybody he was becoming. He was as bad as Marie Murkin. Let her fret about such things. Which, he found when he went down to supper, was just what she had been doing.

"Liz Mortimer and that professor are an item, aren't they?"

"In what sense?"

"You must have noticed the way he looks at her."

"How does he look at her?"

"The way a man looks at a woman." Marie was resolved to be patient with his feigned obtuseness.

"And does she look at him in the way a woman looks at a man?"

"It's not the same thing."

"How does it differ?"

"A woman doesn't *look*. She's looked *at*."

"I see."

He kept a straight face, but Marie knew he was teasing.

"I noticed him looking at you, Marie."

She tucked in her chin and glared at him.

"The way a man looks at a woman, too."

"You're impossible." She stomped into the kitchen, making the door swing to and fro for half a minute after she was gone.

"I think they'll wait until after the funeral," he said musingly, but in a carrying voice. From the kitchen came the sound of pans banging against one another, and then water began to run violently.

23

Carl's mother told him that Alice Mortimer was dead, and Janet and Anne went on about it, how old she had been, how it had happened, with his mother saying things about how Alice had gone off to Chicago when she was just out of high school. Carl had the feeling they didn't want him around, so he went to his room and booted up his computer. But then he stared at the cursor blinking on the screen and could almost see the words appear there, black on white: Alice Mortimer was murdered. Alice Mortimer is dead.

It was the first time someone he had known, had actually talked to, had died. It was a strange feeling. He had served as an altar boy at several funerals, carrying the censer from which clouds of sweet-smelling smoke arose after Father Dowling sprinkled incense on the smoldering cakes of charcoal. Carl would lower the lid over the censer, manipulating the chains that lowered the lid, then hand it to the priest, who would move slowly around the casket, tracing crosses over it with puffs of smoke. From time to time Carl would glance at the mourners in the pews. But it was all something of which he had no real understanding.

What if he were to be an altar boy at Alice Mortimer's funeral? That would be something! He found himself recalling the times he had seen her, the things she had said. He remembered her first visit, with the man named Salvatore Bianco. It did not surprise Carl that the police had arrested him. Carl could imagine that man killing someone the way he might slap at a mosquito.

Mrs. Mortimer had been frightened of him. Maybe she would have enjoyed her daughter's visit if he hadn't been there, but he'd spoiled it, and no wonder. And then Alice had come back alone. Carl remembered that day when she had gone into the house and not come out for a long time, even though he'd told her her mother wasn't there.

She'd been looking for something, he was sure of it. Coming with that man Salvatore, then coming back alone, and then the other time, she had been looking for something.

He thought of the little red envelope Mrs. Mortimer had had him hide in the garage. Was that what Alice had been after? Now that she was dead, it seemed pretty important. All that looking around and now she was dead, and what difference would it have made if she had found the envelope?

But what if she had found it? What if she and that giant found it and that was why Alice had been killed?

"I'm going to ride my bike, Mom."

"Be back in a hour."

"An hour!"

"You know what I mean."

Riding to Mrs. Mortimer's, he wondered if he should check first to see if the key was there. He could come up the alley and get into the garage without being seen and look in the cabinet behind the window rack. The envelope could be gone and Mrs. Mortimer not even know about it. If it was gone, the police should be told, because it would help them explain what had happened to Alice. Obviously that envelope was important, and just as obviously Mrs. Mortimer had wanted it to be a secret.

He decided to talk to Mrs. Mortimer first. Remembering the last time he had come up the alley and hidden in the cardboard box, only to be tipped over by Lieutenant Horvath, had something to do with his change of mind.

When Mrs. Mortimer opened the door, she immediately took him in her arms and hugged him to her, then led him into the house. He realized that she was crying, and knowing what had happened to her daughter, he felt sorry for her; but he sure wished she would release him from her bear hug. She was even running her fingers through his hair. Carl began to wish he hadn't come. Finally she let him go.

"I think I know why she was killed, Mrs. Mortimer."

Mrs. Mortimer looked as if she were going to cry again.

"It's the envelope you asked me to hide. . . ."

Her finger flew to her lips, and she shook her head. Silence fell, and she seemed to be listening. After a moment she spoke, but she sounded as though she were talking to someone else.

"It was very considerate of you to come, Carl. The next few days will be confusing ones. . . ."

"I have to mow the lawn tomorrow." For a moment he feared that what had happened would be the end of his summer job.

"Good. I want you to do that."

Professor Coburn came into the room then, bringing a glass of iced tea for Mrs. Mortimer. He seemed to ignore Carl until Mrs. Mortimer mentioned him.

"You remember Carl Hospers, Richard. He came to pay his respects." Her voice trembled, and she brought her hand to her mouth. Coburn helped her onto a chair.

"Of course I remember Carl."

He turned and advanced on Carl, hand extended, and then Carl felt his hand enveloped by Professor Coburn's huge ones. They were smooth and cool and could have crushed his like a soda can.

Carl felt dumb for having mentioned the envelope before knowing whether anyone might be listening. The thing was supposed to be a secret between him and Mrs. Mortimer. But Professor Coburn seemed not to have heard. In fact, Mrs. Mortimer had to repeat her suggestion that he bring Carl something. Carl hoped the huge old professor was hard of hearing.

"I have to get home, Mrs. Mortimer."

"Thank you again, Carl." She beckoned him closer, and again she hugged him. Carl avoided looking up at Professor Coburn.

Outside, he rolled his bike down to the sidewalk before getting on, and as he started off he thought of that hidden envelope. He rode away but at the corner turned and then turned again, coming back through the alley. A car was coming toward him, and he got off his bike and pushed it to give the car plenty of room in the narrow alley. He was still pushing it when he got to the Mortimer backyard. He had stopped and pulled his bike back out of sight when he saw that Mrs. Mortimer and Professor Coburn had come out of the house and were settling onto chairs on the back lawn. It was as secluded there as in the house, and on a day like this it was a shame to be inside.

Professor Coburn fussed over Mrs. Mortimer, getting her comfortable. He acted as if he thought she were an invalid. Maybe it was because he was such a big man, but Carl thought his hovering over the fragile old lady was more of a threat than a comfort.

24

"We can't hold him," said Ternan, the assistant prosecutor. He had a pencil crosswise in his mouth and reminded Cy of a horse in the chariot race in *Ben-Hur*.

"With his record?" Phil Keegan cried.

It was an old story, the debate between detectives and prosecutors. Police looked for evidence because they were pretty sure someone had committed a crime, but the prosecutor needed evidence before he could arraign someone for a crime.

"His driver's license is a year out-of-date."

Ternan just looked at Cy. "Is that the charge?"

"Quintin, this guy killed that woman. He's a killer."

"He's got no convictions."

"Do you? Do you want a hit man like that just walking out of here?"

Listening, Cy could too easily see Ternan's side. The prosecutor couldn't convince a judge and jury if they couldn't convince the prosecutor. From their point of view, it was so welcome to have a guy like Salvatore Bianco in jail on any excuse, they didn't want to let him go.

"What's the motive?" Ternan asked.

Cy got Phil Keegan out of there. This was not an argument they could win. They didn't deserve to win it, not without more commanding evidence. But it was Ternan's last question that stuck in Cy's mind. What was the motive? Why would Salvatore Bianco kill Alice Mortimer?

Because someone told him to. That would be the only answer that fit their estimate of the man. Keegan wanted him kept in jail because they *knew* Sal Bianco was a muscle man for the mob, and sometimes that meant killing. Was that what they were saying now?

"Go get some evidence," Phil said angrily when they parted.

"Sorry I got you into that."

"Hey." Phil took his arm. "I knew we wouldn't win. But it was important to express our estimate of Bianco. If we treated him like a traffic violator, that's how the prosecutor's office would start thinking of him."

"I'll tell him to get his driver's license renewed."

"Yeah."

Cy didn't stick around to watch Sal Bianco walk away a free man. He wouldn't be the first criminal who had escaped punishment. But what if the gorilla was innocent?

Bianco was a suspect because he had been seen recently with Alice Mortimer. Her mother had feared he was her daughter's fiancé, but Bianco already had a wife. Was that the problem? That he'd had one too many women and had to get rid of one? It was usually one rival who got rid of the other. Cy thought of mousy little Sylvia Bianco, then shook the thought away. Killing to keep Bianco didn't sound like much of a motive. So, had Bianco killed Alice to get rid of a complication in his life?

But why imagine, as Mrs. Mortimer had, that there was a romantic connection between Alice and Bianco? Sure, he had come to the house with her several times, but imagine it was business. What was business for Sal Bianco? The interests of his employers who controlled the rackets. Gambling. Mr. Mortimer had been a gambler, had won big before he'd died. . . .

Orestes Wirth had played football with Cy in high school. He had also had a college career and two years in the pros before he took the job at First Fox River, where he was now a vice president. Cy reminded Orestes of his title when he got him on the phone.

"Cy, everyone who isn't a teller is a vice president."

"I know this is Sunday, but this is urgent."

"What difference does it make if you don't find out until tomorrow morning?"

"I can't divulge that." Cy crossed his fingers.

In the end, Orestes agreed to go to the bank and check on the Mortimer account. When he called it was evening, but Cy was happy to go the bank and hear what Orestes had found out.

"Does that help, Cy?"

"You sure that's all?"

"That's all she has with us."

"Her husband wouldn't still have an account?"

"This is the only Mortimer account. What's it all about, Cy?"

"What would you do if you won a very large sum gambling?"

"And got paid in cash? Well, the tax would be taken out before they'd hand the money over. The IRS makes house calls in such a case. Indeed, they're at the bank all the time. I don't know. Maybe put it in a safe-deposit box."

"Does Mrs. Mortimer have a safety-deposit box?"

"I thought you'd never ask."

"What's in it?"

"You know I can't help you there, Cy. Why don't you ask the lady?"

"You sure she knows about this?"

"It's in her name."

"Has she ever looked at it?"

"What are you getting at?"

"Would it have been possible for her husband to rent that box in her name, put something in it, and not tell her about it?"

Orestes didn't like the suggestion that people could play such games with his bank's safety-deposit boxes. "I'll repeat myself. Why don't you ask the lady?"

"Don't you have records?"

"I wondered if you'd ask that."

"Do you?"

"They're confidential, Cy."

"You can't show them to me."

"No."

"All right. Then you look and tell me if Mrs. Mortimer ever asked to see that box."

Orestes thought about it. Technically this would be a violation of bank rules. But a rule of confidentiality was one thing, helping the law in the investigation of a criminal matter was another.

Orestes turned and walked out of his office to where the person in charge of the safety-deposit boxes had her desk. He made a few deft movements on the keyboard of her computer, frowned, and pulled open a desk. He took out a small metal box. It contained three-by-five index cards, one for each box, recording when the renter asked to see his box, with the date rubber stamped and then the signature of the user. The time in and time out were written in a spidery hand.

"Hortense," Orestes said with bemused impatience. "She hates computers. This is the system that was used when she came to work here, and she still uses it."

Meanwhile he was flipping through the cards. Cy tried to look over his shoulder, but Orestes moved, cutting the cards from view. Then he was putting the box back into the drawer.

"I'll show you out."

"Well?"

"Yes."

"Meaning Mrs. Mortimer herself has signed in to look at her safety-deposit box."

"Once."

"Thanks, Orestes."

"Not at all. Anytime someone comes asking to look at your financial records, I will be happy to oblige them."

"Be my guest."

Holding the door open, Orestes peered at him. "Don't you bank here?"

"We have a checking account."

"No savings!"

"Just my pension."

"There ought to be a law."

"There is. It's called supply and demand."

25

Professor Coburn came out of the house, stood for a moment, breathing deeply and smiling at the world, and then began to walk slowly, hands clasped behind his back. He hadn't looked at Carl, but Carl still had the sense the professor had come out to see him.

Coburn stopped halfway down the drive and, hands still behind his back, looked up and down the street as if he had never noticed it before. Where he was standing was where Carl would be if he kept the lawn mower on its present line. Abruptly he turned the machine and started toward the street, at right angles to his original direction. He liked to follow different patterns when he mowed—sometimes back and forth from house to street, sometimes across the yard, from side to driveway, as he had been doing, sometimes diagonally. Out of the corner of his eye, he saw that Professor Coburn had begun to stroll again. Soon he was coming along the sidewalk toward Carl. Carl pushed the mower toward the house and then turned again and headed toward the driveway.

"Carl!"

It was Professor Coburn. Carl pretended that the noise of the mower and his concentration on his work prevented him from hearing. He had almost reached the driveway when a hand closed around his arm, stopping him.

"I called you." Despite the tightness of his grip, Professor Coburn smiled kindly at Carl.

"Oh."

"You didn't hear me?"

"What do you want?"

Coburn let go of his arm, put his hands behind his back again, and looked at the odd pattern Carl had just described on the grass.

"Mowing gets pretty boring, I imagine."

"I like it."

"I heard you mentioning an envelope to Mrs. Mortimer."

Carl knitted his brow and looked dumb.

"An envelope you put in a safe place for her."

Carl said nothing.

"Where is it?"

"Won't Mrs. Mortimer tell you?"

The smile was gone, and again Coburn got a grip on Carl's arm. He spoke very low but quite distinctly. "Show me where you hid that envelope."

"I have to finish the yard!"

"Is it here?"

Carl shook his head, but he knew that even if he didn't say anything, he was lying. Only it didn't feel like lying. Wouldn't it be worse to tell Coburn where that envelope was? Mrs. Mortimer had stopped him from talking about it because she'd thought Coburn would hear. Well, he had. He should ask Mrs. Mortimer, not pick on a kid and put him on such a spot—either lie or betray Mrs. Mortimer.

"Mrs. Mortimer likes you, Carl. She treats you like her grandson. Do you like her?"

Carl did not answer. The expression in Professor Coburn's eyes was like that he he had seen in Salvatore Bianco's.

"Of course you do. That is why you must tell me where that key is. When I asked Mrs. Mortimer, she had an attack. We should give her her pills, Carl. Otherwise . . ." He looked away for a moment, and then his dead fish eyes were on Carl again and the grip on Carl's arm tightened. "Where is that envelope?"

Mrs. Mortimer was more valuable than a stupid envelope.

"In the garage!"

"Show me."

"Behind the windows. You can find it. I'll go inside."

But Professor Coburn was propelling him around the house and across the backyard toward the garage. Carl had left the door open when he'd gotten the lawn mower, and soon they were inside, where it was cool and smelled of oil and grease and gasoline. Carl was desperate to get free of Coburn now. He began to pull out the racked storm windows with his free hand, and then Coburn let go of his arm and began to help.

"That cabinet behind," Carl said.

Coburn brushed him aside and, big as he was, crawled in behind the windows. He got to his feet in the narrow space, and his hand reached for the cabinet handle. That was when Carl shoved the windows back into place, pushing them as hard as he could, ignoring the sharp cry of pain from Coburn as the windows pinned him against the closed door of the cabinet. Carl dashed outside, pulled down the garage door, and turned the key in the lock. Then he was running toward the house. He ran right into Father Dowling, whose car was parked in the driveway.

"Come on," Carl called, going into the house.

Mrs. Mortimer sat on the couch, very still. She did not look at him when he burst into the living room. She was very pale. Her hand seemed to have stopped on its way to her throat. And then he realized that she was dead.

Father Dowling realized it, too. He stood over her and murmured some prayers. Carl waited until he was done.

"Professor Coburn is locked in the garage, Father."

Father Dowling nodded and picked up the telephone.

26

When Cy Horvath unlocked the garage he found Professor Coburn standing amid a chaos of broken storm windows. He was gripping a small red envelope in his hand. He backed into the dark.

"I can explain," he said.

"Good."

Father Dowling and Carl were in the backyard; there was a patrol car in the alley and another at the curb, and Cy's car was in the driveway

"I can explain," Coburn said to Father Dowling as Cy hustled him toward the driveway.

He had a story, if not an explanation. Cy listened to it, twice, then Phil Keegan and Father Dowling had the professor start from scratch and listened to it. Coburn's story was that Liz had had a seizure and before he could get her pills, she was gone. Then he remembered her remark to Carl and went outside to talk to the boy.

"You thought she was dead?"

"There was no doubt of that."

"And you just left her there."

"There was nothing anyone could do."

"Do you have a medical degree?"

"Captain, I know a dead body when I see one."

Maybe if he hadn't insisted on that, they would have concentrated on breaking his story about how Liz Mortimer had died.

"As dead as Harry Mortimer?" Father Dowling asked.

"Yes, yes." Coburn's gaze lingered on Father Dowling. "You officiated at his funeral."

"As dead as Willy Hanson?"

"Poor Willy."

"Another accident."

"He slipped on the ice."

"Another rival gone?" Cy put in.

"Why don't you tell us the whole story, Coburn?"

"The whole story?"

"Get it off your conscience, Professor," Father Dowling said. "It's all over."

But at that point Coburn might have escaped responsibility for the other deaths. If he had refused to talk, there was only the flimsiest of evidence and much conjecture to justify the larger story. Perhaps it was the instinct of the teacher that undid Richard Coburn, the desire to lecture, to instruct, to inform. And there was a perverse pride in his voice, too, as if he knew that without his cooperation, his deeds might go unpunished.

He had killed Willy. He had walked with him out to the parking lot and then, in a trick he remembered from boyhood, had shot his foot at Willy's, knocking his feet from under him on the icy surface. The sound of his head hitting the ice still seemed audible to Coburn.

"I pulled him to the edge of the lot," Coburn said, and added, "He might have been run over otherwise."

He had seen Willy as his rival for the money Liz

Mortimer had inherited from her good-for-nothing husband. How had he found out? The chatterbox guard at the college, a man named Wexford. He had bided his time. His first effort to interest Liz in himself had been unsuccessful, but he'd been unable to forget the money. Liz's lifestyle made it clear that she was living only on her retirement pension. Imagine his alarm when the daughter had showed up on the scene. Here was another rival. He had wanted her dead before he visited Liz and received her answer to his written proposal of marriage.

The great surprise was Coburn's revelation that he had been responsible for the death of Harry Mortimer as well.

"When I heard of the fortune he had won, I had to act quickly. He could lose it as fast as he had won it."

Coburn seemed satisfied with himself when he was through, looking about as if for at least grudging admiration.

"And all for naught," Father Dowling murmured.

Coburn's face clouded. "I would have succeeded, except . . ."

"Except for Carl," Father Dowling said.

All his pride deserted Coburn, and he seemed to sink into himself. When he was taken away, he was only another foolish, defeated man who had thought the lives of others were in his power to take with impunity.

Carl served at Mrs. Mortimer's funeral, assisted by Gerry Krause, Captain Keegan's nephew. The mourners were the old people from the parish center. The deceased had no living relatives. Her only daughter had been buried from the parish in which her apartment was located, although the priest there had never seen her before. Father Dowling assured him that Alice Mortimer deserved a Christian burial.

When they returned from the cemetery, Gerry went off to the school with Janet.

"I guess I've lost my summer job," Carl said.

"I've been thinking about that," Father Dowling said. "I think it's about time we started using computers in the rectory. Maybe you could give me some pointers on what to buy and then get them set up properly."

Carl was delighted and within a week had turned one of the small parlors into a computing center, somewhat to Marie Murkin's dismay. The computer reminded her of a microwave oven, which she would have in her kitchen only over her dead body. But she was in the parlor with Father Dowling, watching Carl load the programs, when the call came from the bank. It was Orestes Wirth. Mrs. Mortimer's safe-deposit box had been opened in the presence of various officials, including those from the IRS.

"They were satisfied that taxes have already been paid on the money, Father Dowling. It is a considerable sum."

"How much?"

"One hundred and seventy-five thousand dollars."

"Good heavens."

"An appropriate remark, as it happens. There was a note in the box as well. Mrs. Mortimer has left the money to the St. Hilary Parish Center."